LAST FRIENDS

LAST FRIENDS

JANE GARDAM

Little, Brown

LITTLE, BROWN

First published in Great Britain in 2013 by Little, Brown

Copyright © Jane Gardam 2013

The moral right of the author has been asserted.

A CIP catalogue record for this book
is available from the British Library.

Hardback ISBN 978-1-4087-0367-0
C-Format ISBN 978-1-4087-0439-4

Typeset in Sabon by M Rules
Printed and bound in Great Britain by
Clays Ltd, St Ives plc

Papers used by Little, Brown are from well-managed forests
and other responsible sources.

MIX
Paper from
responsible sources
FSC® C104740

Little, Brown
An imprint of
Little, Brown Book Group
100 Victoria Embankment
London EC4Y 0DY

An Hachette UK Company
www.hachette.co.uk

www.littlebrown.co.uk

Contents

To Peter Burton, and also to Harland Walshaw,
and to Mary Sill.
Friends ever.

PART ONE:

Dorset

Chapter One

The Titans were gone. They had clashed their last. Sir Edward Feathers, affectionately known as Filth (Failed In London, Try Hong Kong), and Sir Terence Veneering, the two greatest exponents of English and International Law in the engineering and construction industry and the current experts upon the Ethics of Pollution, were dead. Their well-worn armour had fallen from them with barely a clatter and the quiet Dorset village to which they had retired within a very few years of each other (accidentally, for they had hated one another for over fifty years) mourned their passing and wondered who would be distinguished enough to buy their houses.

How they had hated! For over half a century they had been fetching up all over the world, eyeball to eyeball, Hector and Achilles, usually on battlefields far from home, championing or rubbishing – depending on the client – great broken bridges, mouldering reservoirs, wild crumbling new roads across mountain ranges, sewage works, wind farms, ocean barrages and the leaking swimming pools of moguls. That they had in old age finished up by buying houses next door to each other in a village where there was absolutely nothing to do must have been the result of something the lolling gods had set up one drab day on Olympus to give the legal world a laugh.

And the laugh had been uneasy, because it had been said for years – well, everyone knew – that Edward Feathers' dead wife, Betty, had been the lover of Sir Terry. Or maybe not exactly the lover. But something. There had been something between them. Well, there had been love.

Elisabeth – Betty – Feathers had died some years before the arrival of Sir Terry next door.

Her husband, Old Filth, Sir Edward, the great crag of a man seated above her on the patio pretending to shoot rooks with his walking-stick, a gin and tonic at his elbow, had been left, quite simply, broken-hearted.

Birds and beasts were important to Old Filth. Donkeys' years ago his prep-school headmaster had taught him about birds. It was birds and the language of the natural world and the headmaster, whose name was briefly 'Sir', who had cured him of his awful childhood stammer and enabled him to become an advocate.

His house, Dexters, lay in a long narrow dell off the village hill, bird-haunted and surrounded by trees. Beyond his gate, up the same turn-off and out of sight, Veneering's house stood at the top of the view. Veneering's taller, darker trees hung over the lane but the rooks ignored them. Rooks, thought Old Filth, choose their friends. They will only abandon a friend if they have foreknowledge of disaster. Each night before sleep and each morning, Filth lay in his bed straight as a sentry, striped Chilprufe pyjamas neatly buttoned, handkerchief in breast pocket carefully folded, and listened to the vigorous clamour of the rooks and was comforted. So long as he could hear their passionate disputations he would never miss his life at the Commercial Bar.

He did rather wish they had been cleaner birds. Their nests were old and huge. Ramshackle and filthy. Filth himself was ostentatiously clean. His fingernails and toenails were pearly (chiropodist to the house every sixth week: twenty-five pounds a time), his hair still not grey but curly, autumnal bronze. His complexion shone and was scarcely lined. He smelled – rather excitingly – of Wright's coal-tar soap, a commodity beginning to be rare in many parts of the country.

'He must have had something to hide,' said young barristers. 'Something nasty in his wood shed.' 'What, Old Filth!' they cried. 'Impossible!' They were of course wrong. Eddie Feathers QC had as much to hide as everybody else.

But whatever it was, it would have nothing to do with money. He never mentioned the stuff. He was a gentleman to the end. There must have been buckets of it somewhere. Bucket upon bucket upon bucket, thanks to the long, long international practice. And he spent nothing, or nothing much. Maybe a bit more than the mysterious Veneering next door. Filth was not a vain man. He strode about the lanes in expensive tweeds, but they were very old. Not much fun, but never pompous. If he ever brooded upon his well-organised millions, managed by impeccable brokers, he didn't think about them much. He joked about them occasionally. 'Oh yes, I have "held the gorgeous East in fee",' he would say, 'ha-ha', quoting Sir, his headmaster.

He himself never went to the theatre or read poetry, for he wept too easily.

After a time a lethargy had fallen upon Filth. He lost the energy even to think about moving house. And maybe the old enemy up the slope had begun to feel the same. They never met. If occasionally they found themselves passing one another at a distance during an afternoon walk in the lanes, each looked away.

Then, after a year or so, something must have happened. It was never discussed, even in the village shop, but there were some astonishing sightings, sounds of old English accents, staccato in the bluebell woods. It happened over a snow-bound Christmas. Before long it was reported that the two old buffers were playing chess together on Thursdays. And when Terry Veneering died during a ridiculous jaunt – foot in a hole on a clifftop on the island of Malta and then thrombosis – Edward Feathers said, 'Silly old fool. Far too old for that sort of thing. I told him so,' but was surprised how much he missed him.

Yet he refused to attend Veneering's memorial service at Temple Church in London. There would have been comment and Betty's name bandied about. For all his Olympian manner, Old Filth was not histrionic. Never. He stayed alone at home that day, making notes on the new edition of *Hudson's Building and Engineering Contracts* that he had been (flatteringly, considering his age) asked to re-edit some years before. He had a whisky and a slice of ham for his supper and listened to the news. When he heard the returning cars of the village mourners passing the end of his lane from Tisbury Station he sensed disapproval at his absence like a wet cloth across the face; and turned a page.

Nobody came to see him that evening, not even sexy old Chloe who was never off his doorstep with shepherd's pies. Not his gardener nor his cleaning lady who had travelled to the memorial service in London and back together in the gardener's pick-up. Not Dulcie who lived near by on Privilege Hill and was just about his oldest friend, the widow of an endearing old Hong Kong judge dead years ago and much lamented. Dulcie was a tiny, rather stupid woman, and *grande dame* of the village.

'Let them think what they like,' said Old Filth into his double malt. 'I am past all these frivolities.'

But the next frivolity was to be his own, for the following Christmas he took himself off alone to the place of his birth, which he still called the Malay States, and died as he stepped off the plane.

Chapter Two

And so, on a cold morning in March the Dorset village of Donhead St Ague was off to its second memorial service within a few months, the first having been for Veneering, the second for Filth, off to Temple Church again, waiting for the London train on Tisbury Station. In prime positions were a group of three and a group of four, all sombrely and correctly dressed but standing at different ends of the platform because although they were neighbours they were not yet exactly friends.

The group of four had recently bought Veneering's house, invisible from the road but known for its brashness and flamboyance and ugliness like its old owner and, like its old owner, keeping out of sight. They were father, mother, son and daughter, most *ordinary* people, it was said, though it was vaguely thought that the father was some sort of intellectual.

Waiting at the front end of the train was the elder of the village: old Dulcie the widow, with her daughter Susan and her twelve-year-old grandson Herman, an American child, serious and very free with his opinions. Dulcie was half his size, a tiny woman in grey moleskin and a hat made of what could have been the feathers of the village rooks. It was a hat bought forty years ago in Bond Street for the Queen's birthday in Dar es Salaam, where Dulcie's husband had been an easygoing and contented judge even at a hanging.

Susan, Dulcie's stocky daughter, was a glum person, married to an invisible husband who seldom stirred from Boston, Massachusetts. Granny, mother and son were about to travel first class in reserved seats.

The group of four, who had never reserved a seat for anything in their lives, were stamping noisily about, waiting to fight their way into the last carriage, quite ready to stand all the way to Waterloo among the people who'd been down to Weymouth for the Bank Holiday and would be drunk or drugged or singing and drinking smoothies, some of the tattooed young men wearing dresses. These old Dulcie would somehow be spared. She had a heart murmur.

The group of three settled themselves in first class. Susan began to demolish the *Daily Telegraph* crossword, flung it from her completed within minutes and said, 'I don't know why we're going. We're hardly over Veneering's.'

'Oh, *I* am,' said Dulcie. 'I quite enjoyed it.'

'It's not good for you, Ma. All this death. At your age.'

'Oh, I don't know,' said Dulcie. 'It keeps people in touch.'

'I'm not keen on touching people.'

'I know, dear,' said Dulcie, looking at her grandson and wondering how ever he had come into the world.

'I don't suppose there'll be anyone there we'll even remember, you know. Filth was much older than you. You married from the schoolroom.'

'Did I? Good gracious,' said Dulcie.

'Ma,' said Susan, and amazingly touched her mother's hand, 'you mustn't be upset if there's nobody much there. At his age. Veneering was younger.'

*

But surprisingly the church was full. There were young people there – whoever were they? – and people who didn't look at all like lawyers. Groups seemed to be arranging themselves in tribes, nodding and smiling at each other. Some stared with polite surprise, some with distaste. There was a dwarf. Well, of course. He'd been Filth's instructing solicitor for decades – but surely he was dead? Here he was, legs stuck out in front of him, face creased like an old nut, vast brown felt hat on his knee and sitting in one of the lateral seats reserved for Benchers only. And refusing to move.

The intellectual family man whispered to his wife that the dwarf was a celebrity, to tell the children to look at him. 'Must be a hundred. They will tell their grandchildren. Said to have been dead ten times over. Had some sort of power over Filth.' The two children looked unimpressed and the little girl asked if the Queen would be coming.

There was a pew full of generations of a family with the queer pigmentation of ex-pats. Britons – a pale cheese colour, like Wensleydale. There was a row of Straits Chinese and some Japanese who were being reprimanded about their mobile phones. There was a huge sad man rambling about at the back of the church near the medieval knights who lay on the floor with broken swords and noses. 'Barristers?' asked the children, but the intellectual father wasn't sure. The old man was silently refusing to be moved to a more distinguished seat, it having been discovered that he'd once been a Vice-Chancellor.

There was Old Filth's gardener and cleaning lady, who had parked the pick-up in the Temple this time round and had just finished a slap-up lunch at the Cheshire Cheese in the Strand. And there was a very, very old, tall woman, just arriving, sliding in among the Orientals, in a long silk coat – pale rose pink – as the choir and organ set to on the opening hymn.

'I'll bet that was his mistress,' said the intellectual.

'More likely it's her ghost,' said his wife.

And then they all began to sing 'I Vow to Thee My Country', which, for Old Filth, born on the Black River in the jungles of Malaysia, wrapped in the arms of a childish *ayah*, happily rocked by the night sounds of water and trees and invisible creatures and watched over by different gods, had never been England anyway.

Chapter Three

After the service old Dulcie found that she didn't want to stay long at the gathering in Parliament Chamber across Temple Yard. Talk had broken into chorus as they all streamed out. Conversation swelled. The dwarf was being waved off in a splendid car, tossing his hat to the crowd like a hero. Streams of guests were passing up the steps of Inner Temple Hall and towards the champagne. Dulcie clutched Susan's arm; then, inside the chamber, observed people looking uncertainly at each other before plunging. She watched them watching each other furtively, from a distance. She examined – and recognised – the degrees of enthusiasm as they asked a name. She saw some things that had worried her lately. And so much going on besides that she seemed to be seeing for the first time, or analysing for the first time, though she knew that it was everyday, as habitual as looking at the clock or holding out a hand. Yet whatever did it mean?

She was sure that she knew any number of the looming, talkative, exclaiming faces, if she could only brush away the threads and lines that now veiled them. And the curious papery dried-out skin! 'I'm afraid it was all our *cigarettes*,' she said to someone passing by in pale pink silk. The woman immediately melted off-stage. Over in a corner, rowdy people seemed to be passing around the dwarf's hat and a cheer went up. 'Cowboys,' she said. 'It is like a saloon.' She moved towards the lovely long windows, hearing everywhere half-familiar voices and names of old friends lamented for being long gone.

But they were not long gone to her. Oh, never! Since school-days, and just like her mother, Dulcie had kept all her address books and birthday books and a tattered pre-war autograph book. Some of the names, of course, were hazy on the page. Some were firmly crossed out by Susan. ('But there were *always* Vansittarts at Wingfield.' 'Susan, do *not* cross that out. I'll be sending a Christmas card.') I must learn this email, she thought. Tomorrow. 'Susan – could we go home?'

Susan fetched her mother's coat. Naturally Dulcie had kept her hat on. It made for a pleasant, feathery shadow but she had a wish that she were of this generation (who would have left a hat in the cloakroom) and shown that she wasn't going thin on top like most of them; but she didn't quite dare. Her fur coat was expensive and light as wool and smelled of Evening in Paris, setting the odd old nostril quivering as she passed.

A taxi had been called for Waterloo Station and the train home, and Herman was being hunted down. Large and grave, the boy stood looking towards the Thames across Temple Gardens, 'where,' he told his grandmother, 'as I guess you know, they organised the Wars of the Roses.'

'Such lovely lime juice,' said Dulcie, 'and *how* we missed it in the war.'

Herman glowered, saying that clearly only Americans were historians now.

'They have so little of it to learn,' said Dulcie.

'Romantic vista?' asked the ex-Vice-Chancellor, plodding by. 'Hello, Dulcie. I am Cumberledge. Eddie and I were lads together in Wales.'

'Magnificent,' said Dulcie. 'They call it Cumbria now. So affected. Herman darling, I do think it's time to go.'

'The Thames once stank so much they had to move out of the House of Commons,' said Herman.

'Quite a stink there sometimes now,' said a new Queen's Counsel, going by with tipping wineglass.

'I think you should qualify that,' said Herman, but the silk had faded away. 'Granny, nobody's talking to me.'

'Why should they?'

'And there's no music.'

'Well, I don't think Old Filth was – big – on music, darling.'

'Veneering was. I liked Mr Veneering better anyway.'

'So you always say,' said his grandmother. 'I don't know how you know anything about him. And he was Sir Terence. Sir Terry Veneering.'

'Granny, I was nine. He was at your house. His hair was like threads and queer yellow. He played the blues on your piano. Granny, you *must* remember. There was an awful man there too, called Winston Smith or something. Like *1984*. I hope the Winston Smith one's past it, like most of these here. Why's Mr Veneering dead? He noticed me. I'll bet he was an American. They never forget you, Americans. Filthy Feathers' ('Sir Edward,' said Dulcie) 'never had a clue who I was.'

'Taxi now, Herman. Stop talking.'

A little old man seemed to be accompanying them as they left the party.

She had seen him in the church with a second-class railway ticket sticking up from his breast pocket.

When they climbed into their waiting taxi, he climbed in with them. 'Dulcie,' he said, 'I am Fiscal-Smith.'

The name, the face, had been at the rim of Dulcie's perception all day, like the faint trail of light from a dead planet. Fiscal-Smith!

'But,' she said, 'you told me you were never coming to London again after Veneering's party. I mean Memorial. Don't you live somewhere quite North?'

'Good early train. Darlington,' he said. 'My ghillie drove me down from the Hall. Two hours King's Cross. Excellent.'

'What's a ghillie?' asked Herman.

'You know, Dulcie, that I never miss a memorial service. I wouldn't come down for anything else. Well, perhaps for an Investiture ... And you'll remember, I think, that I *was* Old Filth's best man. In Hong Kong. You were there. With Willy.'

'Yes,' said Dulcie – after a pause – her eyes glazing, remembering with terrible clarity that Veneering, of course, had not been present. Not in the flesh.

Fiscal-Smith was never exactly one of us, she thought. No one knows a thing about him now. Jumped up from nowhere. Like Veneering. On the make all his life. In a minute he's going to ask to come back to Dorset with us for a free bed-and-breakfast. He'll be asking me to marry him next.

'I'm nearly eighty-three,' she said, confusing him.

He took his Cheap Day second-class rail ticket from his pocket and read it through. 'I was just thinking,' he said, 'I might come back with you to Dorset? Stay a few nights? Old times? Talk about Willy? Maybe a week? Or two? Possibility?'

In the train he sat down at once in Herman's reserved seat. 'That,' said Herman, 'is not legal.'

'Justice,' said Fiscal-Smith, 'has nothing to do with Law.'

'Well you'll have to help me to get Mother out,' said Susan. 'Tisbury has a big drop.'

'I wouldn't mind a big drop now,' said Fiscal-Smith, 'or even a small one. Will there be a trolley?'

There was not. The journey was tedious. Fiscal-Smith had trouble with the ticket inspector, who was slow to admit that you have a right to a first-class seat with only the return half of a basic Fun Day Special to another part of the country. Fiscal-Smith won the case, as he had been known to do before, through relentless wearing-down of the defence, who went shakily off through the rattletrap doors. 'Ridiculous man. Quite untrained,' said Fiscal-Smith.

The train stopped at last at Tisbury, waiting in the wings for the down-line train to hurtle by. 'Excellent management,' said Fiscal-Smith as they drew up on the platform and the usual *Titanic*-style evacuation took place from its eccentric height, passengers leaping into the air and hoping to be caught. 'Very dangerous,' said Fiscal-Smith. 'Very well known hazard, this line. "Every man for himself."' He then completely disappeared.

Dulcie and Susan were rescued by the intellectual family man, who came running up the platform to take Dulcie in his arms and lift her down.

'How well you can run,' she said to him. 'Your legs are as long as dear Edward's. An English gentleman could always be identified by his long legs, you know, once. Though in old age they all became rather floppy in the shanks.' Seeing suddenly Old Filth's rotting remains in the English cemetery in Dacca and nobody to put flowers on them, her pale eyes filled with tears. Everyone gone now, she thought. Nobody left.

'Come on back with us,' said the family man. 'It's a foul night. I'll drop you at home. We have a car rug.'

But she said, 'No, the family had better stay together. You can have Fiscal-Smith,' she added, which he seemed not to hear.

Fiscal-Smith had already found Susan's old Morris Traveller in the car park and was fussing round it.

'Well, keep our lights in view,' called the family man, who was at once invisible through the murk and lashing rain.

As Susan drove carefully along behind, they all fell silent. They passed Old Filth's empty house, in its hollow, but Dulcie didn't peer down at it. She thought of his steady friendship and noble soul. What Fiscal-Smith was thinking it was hard to say. The car swished through lakes of rain in the road, the deluge and the dark. Dulcie looked straight ahead.

They began to speak again only as they reached Dulcie's stately home on Privilege Hill, where in minutes lights blazed, central heating and hot water were turned up higher, soup, bread and cheese appeared and the telly was switched on for the news.

The smell of deep-blue hyacinths in bowls set heads spinning, and the polished blackness of the windows before the curtains were drawn across showed that the wet and starless world had passed into infinite space. Dulcie thought again about the last scene of the last act.

'Why were all the lights on in his house?' asked Herman.

'Whose house? Filth's?' said Susan. 'They weren't. It's been locked up since Christmas. Chains on the gates.'

'Didn't notice the gates,' said the grandson, 'but the lights were on all over it. In every room. Shining like always. But there seemed to be more than usual. Every window blazing.'

'I expect it has caught fire,' said Fiscal-Smith, searching out Dulcie's drinks cupboard, as old friends are permitted to do.

Chapter Four

The next morning Dulcie awoke in her comfortable, expensive, foam-lined bed with a sense of unrest. Her window was open in the English tradition, two inches at the top for the circulation of refreshing night air (how they had dreamed of it in all their years in Hong Kong) long before the European central heating. In their native English bedrooms, Dulcie and Willy had always eschewed central heating as working-class.

Outside was country silence except for the clatter of an occasional wooden-looking leaf dropping from the *Magnolia grandiflora* and hitting the stone terrace. Her watch said 5 a.m. Excellent! She had slept all night. She was in time for 'Prayer for the Day' on faithful BBC Four, which she still called the Home Service.

Where was she? Was it today they had to go to London to dear Eddie's thing? No, no. They'd done that. Flames, she thought, flames. Ashes to ashes ... and drifted off to sleep again.

*

Quite soon she woke once more, the flames retreating. She trotted downstairs in slippers and her old dressing-gown of lilac silk, feeling a sort of twitch in a back molar. Oh dear. Time for a check-up. So expensive. Own teeth, every one of them. Thanks to Nannie. A full five minutes' brushing morning and night. More than the teeth at yesterday's party . . . Oh, the awful rictus grins! And the *bridges*! You could *see* them. Queen Elizabeth the First who never smiled, sensible woman. The old Queen Mother who never stopped, and should have done. Early-morning tea.

Willy had always made the early-morning tea. Not in Hong Kong, of course. There had been a slender maid then with a tray, smiling. They thought, the Chinese and the Americans, that it was disgusting. Called it 'bed tea'. Oh, Willy! She tried not to think of Willy in case, once again, she found that she had forgotten what he had looked like. Ah – all well. Here he came up the stairs, his fastidious feet, balancing teacups. Deeply thinking. Oh, *Willy*! So many years! I haven't really forgotten what you looked like. '*Pastry* Willy' – but you grew quite weather-beaten after we came Home. It's just, sometimes lately you've grown hazy. Doesn't matter. Changes nothing. I wish we could have a good *talk*, Willy, about money. There doesn't seem to be much of it. I always put the bank letters away in your desk. Very silly of me. I don't open many of them.

Up by the kitchen ceiling, he was watching her, very kindly but non-committally. No need ever to discuss the big things. He knew she was – well – superficial. Hopeless at school. Men love that, Nannie had said. But shrewd, she thought. *Oh*, yes. I'm shrewd. An unshakeable belief in the Church of England and God's mercy, and *duty* and 'routine'. Early-morning tea. Clocks all over the house (fewer now that I've sold the carriage clocks), wound up each Sunday evening after Evensong. Jesus had probably never seen a clock. *Were* there any? She tried to imagine the Son of Man with a wristwatch, all the time putting from her hazy early-morning mind the fact that she couldn't remember Willy at all. 'I can't see your *face*,' she called to the ceiling.

'Come on: hospitality,' said his voice from behind the kitchen curtains.

Tags and watchwords, she thought. That's what all the love and passion comes down to. We never really talked.

And imagine, sex! Extraordinary! I suppose we did it? Susan was a lovely baby.

She made tea from the loose Darjeeling in the black and gold tin and carried up a pretty tray with sugar basin and milk jug.

What am I doing all this *for*, Willy? It's no wonder Susan just thumps down a mug. Our bloody parents. Highest standards. But what of, Willy? Standards of what? Oh! He had vanished again.

Good. He couldn't answer her.

Now then, Fiscal-Smith. Rockingham china for Fiscal-Smith. I bet he lives off pots and shards in Yorkshire. Mugs there, certainly. And I'm still trying to show him the rules.

She tottered up to the guest room and found it empty.

'Fiscal-Smith?' she called.

(What *is* his first name? Nobody ever knew.)

'Hello?'

(That must be sad for him. Nobody ever asking.)

'Hello?'

Silence.

The bed in his room was tidily turned back – his pale pink and white winceyette pyjamas folded on the pillow, his dressing-gown and slippers side by side by an upright chair.

So he'd brought his night things. He'd intended to stay from the start. The old chancer!

Except that he was absent.

She sat down on his bed and thought: He says he comes in honour of Filth and yet all he wants is to be looked after here. That's all he's after. Being *looked* after. You were so different, Willy. And now all I want is someone to deal with those letters. (My slippers! Time for new slippers.) And peace and quiet. And – absolute silence.

There was a most unholy crash from below stairs.

As she shrieked, she remembered that she was not alone. There were others in the house. Left over from yesterday. She couldn't actually remember the end of yesterday. Any yesterday. The evening before had nowadays usually slipped away by morning. King Lear, poor man ...

But last night hadn't there been something rather sensational? Rather terrible? Oh dear, yes. Poor Old Filth's empty house had burned to the ground. Or something of the sort.

She looked at her feet. Yes, it was time for new slippers. Then through the window she saw Fiscal-Smith tramping up the hill towards her, from the direction of Filth's house, still in yesterday's funeral suit, and he was looking jaunty. Eighty-plus. And plus. Five-thirty a.m. Beginning to rain.

He saw her and called out, 'All well. It's still there.'

'What?'

'Filth's nice old place. The boy was wrong. No sign of fire. I've a feeling that boy is a *stirrer*. He was a stirrer years ago at that lunch you gave. A little monkey!'

'Do you never forget anything, Fiscal-Smith? What lunch?' A lifetime of lunches. And with – for a wobbly second she forgot her grandson's name ... When? Where?

'Two fat sisters. And a priest. And Veneering, of course. Oh, I forget nothing. Mind never falters. It is rather a burden to me, Dulcie.'

'How arrogant you are, Fiscal-Smith.'

'I simply "put my case",' he said.

He was with her in the kitchen now. She said, 'Your case is in your bedroom. Do you want help with packing?' – and shocked herself.

There fell a silence as he stepped out upon the terrace with his cup of tea.

At the same moment, down in Old Filth's house in the dell, Isobel Ingoldby, wrapped now in his Harrod's dressing-gown instead of her own pink silk coat, was turning off the lights which she had left burning all night. Foolish, she was thinking, I'm the one paying for the electricity now. Until I sell. Why did I light the whole place up through the dark? Some primitive thing about the spirit finding its way home? But he won't be searching. His spirit is free. It's back in his birthplace. It maybe never quite left it.

She boiled a kettle for tea but forgot to make any. She wandered about. Betty's favourite chair they had all talked about – God knows why – stood wrapped in a tarpaulin up in the hall. Filth's present for Fiscal-Smith. Nobody gave Fiscal-Smith presents.

This house – the house she had inherited – watched her as she went about. So tidy. So austere. So dead. Betty's photograph on a mantelpiece, fallen over sideways.

Isobel had slept in his bed last night. Someone had removed the sheets and she had lain on the bare mattress with rugs over her. She thought of the first time she'd seen him naked in bed. He had looked about fourteen years old. He was terrified. We both knew, then. I was only his schoolfriend's older cousin, but we recognised each other. All our lives.

Fiscal-Smith still stood on Dulcie's terrace half an hour later, still examining the view over the Roman road towards

Salisbury, the wintry sun trying to enliven the grey fields through the rain.

Dulcie came walking past him towards the wrought-iron gates, fully dressed now in tweed skirt and cardigan, remarkably high heels and some sort of casual coat, not warm, from the cupboard under the stairs. She carried a prayer book. Po-faced.

Fiscal-Smith shouted, 'Where are you going? Filth's house is perfectly all right.'

'I am going to church.'

'Dulcie, it's six o'clock in the morning. It is clouding over. It's beginning to rain. That coat you had in Hong Kong. And it isn't Sunday.' He came up close to her.

'I need to say my prayers.'

'It will be locked.'

'I doubt it. The great Chloe is supposed to open it but she usually forgets to shut and lock it the night before.'

'The mad woman who runs about with cakes?'

'Yes. Well-meaning, but the mind's going. Sometimes she locks in the morning and unlocks at night. We shall have to tell the churchwarden soon. Actually I think she may *be* the churchwarden. There's nothing much going on in the church. Not even anybody sleeping rough. It's too damp . . .'

He was padding along behind her.

'There you are,' she said. 'Unlocked. Unlocked all night.'

Inside, the church scowled at them and blew a blast of damp breath. Hassocks looked ready to sprout moss and there was the hymn-book smell. Notices curled on green baize gone ragged, and the stained-glass windows appeared to bulge inwards from the flanking walls. Two sinister ropes dangled in the belfry tower. It was bitterly cold.

'Stay there,' Dulcie ordered him, making for a chancel

prayer desk up near the organ. 'I can't pray with anyone watching.'

'The Muslims can,' he said, trying to bring the blood back to his knobbed hands. 'This is a refrigerator, not a church.'

'*Muslims*,' she said, 'can crowd together on mats and swing about and keep their circulation going, and you don't see what the women do but I don't think they pray like the men, in a huddle. Anyway, I need what I know,' and she vanished, eastwards.

'Five minutes,' he shouted after her as her high heels tapped out of sight. 'Utter madness,' he said to the stained-glass windows. 'Hopeless woman. Hopeless village.' His own voice echoed hopelessly around the rood screen and its sad saints. Rows of regimental flags drooped down the side-aisle like shredding dishcloths, still as sleeping bats. 'They're all off their heads here,' he called out. There was the sound of a heavy key being turned in the lock of the south door, just behind him. The door by which they had entered.

He sprang towards it, flung himself first through the wire, then through the baize door to the south door they had just pushed heavily through. He tugged and shouted.

But the door was now firmly and determinedly locked from the outside. Chloe, on her bike, had been thinking that it was evening again.

Up in the chancel there was no sign of Dulcie, but at length he saw the top of her head and her praying hands. She was like a – what was it called? A little Dutch thing. Little painting on wood.

Praying hands, he thought. They have them on Christmas cards. Dürer. The Germans were perfectly all right then.

Her head was bowed (she still has thick, curly hair).

'Five minutes,' he called, like a tout, or an invigilator.

Soon he began to hum a tune from his seat in front of the choir-stall, and after a minute she opened angry eyes.

'We are locked in,' he said.

'Nonsense,' she said.

'I heard the key thrust in and turned. It was Chloe.'

Dulcie went pattering back down the central aisle, tried the oak door first with one hand, then the other, then both hands together. She regarded the broad and ancient lock. 'You heard her? Chloe?'

'Yes.'

'Why didn't you shout?'

'I think I did. Now, leave all this to me, Dulcie. I banged and rattled and yelled. I will do it again.'

'Yes. She *is* getting deaf.'

They stood in icy shadow and he called again, 'Hello?'

'It's no good shouting, Fiscal-Smith. Nobody in the village is up yet except Chloe.'

But he roared out: 'Hello *there*! There may be someone walking a dog?'

'Nobody walks a dog as early as this in winter. We are all old here.'

'I'm tired of this "old",' said Fiscal-Smith. 'We don't have it in the North. Won't Susan be coming by on the horse? And where's that boy?'

'Sleeping. And Susan won't be out for at least two hours. She may notice we are missing, but I don't think so.'

'I *suppose*,' he said, 'you don't carry such a thing as a mobile telephone?'

'Good heavens, no. Do you?'

'Never.'

'We could try shouting louder.'

And so they did for a time – treble and bass – but there was no response.

'Of course, there are the bells,' said Dulcie. She was shaking now with cold. 'It might warm us up.'

Fiscal-Smith released the tufted, woolly bell-ropes from their loops in the tower and handed one to her, icy to the touch. She closed her eyes and dragged at it with childish fists. It did not stir.

'I'll have a go,' he said, and after a time, sulkily, on the edge of outrage, the damp and matted bell-pull began to move stiffly up and down: but Fiscal-Smith looked exhausted.

'Go on, go on,' cried Dulcie, 'you got it up, I think,' and thought: I believe I said something rather *risqué* just then, and giggled.

'This is serious, Dulcie. Don't laugh. Go over there and pull the blue one.'

And so they toiled, and after what seemed to be hours they both heard the sad boom of a bell.

'I think it was only the church clock striking seven,' she said.

'We must go on trying.'

But she couldn't, and made for the chancel again and possible candles on the altar for heat. He followed, but the candles looked like greasy ice and all the little night-lights people light for memorials to the dead were brownish and dry and there were no matches. Dulcie's lips were turning blue now. 'This,' she said, not crossly, 'will be the death of me. We have no warm clothing and between us we are nearly two hundred years old. My mother stayed in bed all the time after eighty. There was nothing wrong with her, but everyone cherished her. All the time.'

Through a door they found a vestry and a wall full of modern pine cupboards, BEQUEATHED, said a plaque, BY ELISABETH FEATHERS. 'I wish she'd bequeathed an electric fire,' said Dulcie.

Inside, the cupboards were crammed full of choirboys' black woollen cassocks, and Fiscal-Smith and Dulcie somehow scrambled into one each. Dulcie said they were damp. But then, over in the priests' vestry nearby, there was treasure. Albs, cottas, chasubles and a great golden embroidered cope beneath a linen cover.

'Wrap it round you,' ordered Fiscal-Smith.

'It's reserved for Easter only,' said Dulcie. 'It's for the Bishop and it's too big. It could go round us both.'

So they both stood inside it, their faces looking out from it alongside.

'My neck is still very cold,' said Dulcie. 'Look, there is the ceremonial mitre and the St Ague stole. This church! This church, you know, was once High. And very well endowed.'

'I can't remember what High is. I'm a Roman Catholic,' said Fiscal-Smith, 'but I'm in favour if High turns up the heat. Remember Hong Kong? No copes there. Too hot. This is very curious headgear, Dulcie. We are becoming ridiculous.'

'I wish this was a monastery,' she said. 'There'd be a supply of hoods.'

'That was because of the tonsures.'

'I'm not surprised. I had terrible tonsils as a girl. Before penicillin, and I wasn't a monk. Wonderful penicillin.'

'I'm lost,' said Fiscal-Smith.

'It was God's reward for us winning the war, penicillin.' (She's bats.) 'Willy used to say that every nation that has ever achieved a great empire blazes up for a moment in its dying fire. Penicillin. I wouldn't have missed our Finest Hour, would you, Fiscal-Smith?'

'I bloody would,' he said. Then, after a silence, 'Look here, Dulcie. Where do they keep the Communion wine?'

*

There came at length a loud knocking on the vestry door into the churchyard. 'Are you in there? An answer please. Are you there? Who are you? A bell tolled.'

'Yes, we are locked into the church. Accidentally. Dulcie is not well. It is very cold. This is Sir Frederick Fiscal-Smith speaking. From the North.'

'Have you tried to open the door?'

'Of course we've tried the bloody door.'

'I mean this door. The vestry door. It's beside you. There is an inside bolt.'

Fiscal-Smith leaned from his princely garment, considered the unobtrusive little modern door, slid open a silken brass bolt and revealed the misty morning. There, in running shorts among the graves, stood the family man.

Out through the doorway, laced across with trails of young ivy, a door which, like Christ's in Holman Hunt's *Light of the World* in St Paul's Cathedral, only opened from within, stepped a pair of ancient Siamese twins in cloth-of-gold, one of them wearing a papal headdress and both of them blue to the gills.

Away down past the churchyard at the foot of the steep-stepped path sped old Chloe on her bicycle, bearing on the handlebars a jam sponge and in her other hand the ancient church key. She called a greeting and waved.

'Just wondered if I'd remembered to unlock. So glad I had.' And pressed on.

In the village shop she said, 'There's something going on in the church. I think it's a pageant.'

Chapter Five

Dulcie had been put to bed by Susan.

Fiscal-Smith, with his overnight case beside him on the terrace, was awaiting transport.

'You might call me a taxi.'

Susan said, 'There are no taxis. I'll drive you to the station. Do you want to say goodbye to Ma?'

'Oh, no thank you.'

'She will not be pleased.'

'Whatever I say or do makes not the least difference to her. I make no difference to anyone.'

'Oh, I'm sure ...'

'All the years we have all known each other, do you know, Susan, I've never actually been invited anywhere. And I was present when Betty saw Veneering for the first time. Party. Filth was like Hyperion. Betty looked like the captain of the school hockey team. Gorgeous Betjeman girl. Stalwart but not joyful.'

'You don't have to tell me this ...'

'As she came into the party she saw Veneering across the room. Hell-raising, blond-yellow hair falling over his face, already half drunk (and with a case starting against Eddie next morning), and I saw him see Betty. He had to get hold of a pillar. White and gold. Fluted. His face became very still and serious. Yes. I saw the beginning of it. The disgraceful love affair.'

'We have five minutes to get to the train. You might catch it. But, you know, you're very welcome . . . ' said Susan, now shaken—

'No, I am not.'

In the train he stood inside the doors on the high step and looked down on Susan. 'No. I am not welcome. But thank you for the lift. Edward and Betty never invited me to stay either. For that lunch at Dulcie's I had to walk in from Salisbury. Seven miles.'

'Oh, Fiscal-Smith,' she said, 'until yesterday you were one of the last friends. Her last and her best.'

'I wonder if she remembers,' he said, 'that I was Edward's best man?'

The doors clashed together, clapping their hands a couple of times. There were some fizzing and knocking sounds and then a long sigh. Then the train clattered off, and Susan stood staring at its disappearing rump, wondering why the ridiculous man cared so much about these people who were dead and hadn't liked him anyway. He'd said in the car that Veneering was the best of them. That Veneering *could* have invited him down here.

'But couldn't you have invited them to *you*? To stay with you up in the North?'

'Not possible,' he had said. 'Anyway, I am the only one who knows Veneering's secrets.'

'Did you never have a wife, Fiscal-Smith?'

'Certainly not,' he had said.

God, thought Susan, these old fruits are boring.

Chapter Six

Anna, the young wife of the poet from the house that had been Veneering's, had been at the village shop that morning at the same time as Chloe, buying bread and milk for breakfast, and she had heard the words 'pageant' and 'church'.

She was interested in the church, and the unlikely Saint Ague, and had been allowed to do something about the vestry. She loved robes and the clergy. She came from a vicarage family and wasn't usual. She was the reason why the brass plates in memory of Betty Feathers shone so bright. What a homely name! Some old villager! Then someone else corrected her and told her about wonderful dead Betty, very distinguished woman, and Anna had thought: Oh Lord, another old dear.

And it was Anna now, the family woman, who put the cope in clean sacking and starched the choirboys' surplices so that they looked like preening swans. Sadly there were only three choirboys now and seldom visible. Or audible.

The old guard predicted that soon this woman (Anna) would be in charge of Altar Frontals, then Communion Silver and Candlesticks (already rumoured to be in her attic). Not, of course, Flowers. Only Betty Feathers had dared take on Flowers unasked. Betty Feathers had not had much to do with churches except in Hong Kong, but she was unbeatable on Flowers. During her mature years at St Ague with her perfect husband Sir Edward (Filth) Feathers, vicars of the parish had been grateful for such a conventional and pleasant woman and nothing churchy about her. You would never guess she might take over. And here, most exceptionally, for most of St Ague was fashionably atheist now, was another. This Anna. 'Labourers,' said the village elders, 'do still seem to keep the vineyard going even late in the day. And for no pay.' Anna had been a godsend at the last Harvest Festival and for the first time in years there had been more than tins of baked beans round the lectern.

There had been a bit of a fuss about Anna surrounding the Easter pulpit with bramble bushes. Not only had she taken them up by the roots (she put them back down her drive-way, later and they thrived) but they had damaged several small children who had come with chocolate eggs and Snow Whites.

Mothers – one or two – enquired if she was interested in the cleaning rota and she said, 'I don't want to push in but if you like we've got a power hose and we could cover the Saxon frieze of "The Wounds of St Ague" in bubble-wrap.'

'Or Elastoplast,' said her husband, the poet, the family man.

In the end, the elders let Anna fix up only the vestry. Just for the present.

'I do not care for "fixing up",' said one of the ex-Flower Committee, now confined, like her twin sister, to a wheelchair. They lived with a carer up the lane and went to church on separate weeks as the carer could take only one at a time.

The vicar, tearing past to the next of his string of churches each Sunday, gave thanks for Anna (whoever she was), prayed for new hassocks and fungicides and a box of matches.

'It will take a hundred grand to deal with the vestry. Half a million to save the church,' said Anna. 'We'll have a go with the power hose.'

St Ague's became Anna's secret passion, her plan for life to supersede (or kill) Chloe. Her heart had gone cold with dread when Chloe, that morning, had said the word 'pageant'.

'Oh, yes,' Chloe had said. 'Scarlet and gold. Robes. Pushing out through that little narrow door. Very queer. Something double-headed. Like black magic. We're wondering if it was art? Your husband seemed to be in charge, Anna. Is he a film director?'

'In *charge?*' she cried. 'I left him in bed.'

'Well, he was in running shorts. And he was either on his mobile or directing, like in a play. His arms going up and down.'

Anna said that she had better get home, but instead launched her car with the breakfast in it towards Privilege House, which seemed to be empty except for Herman, who was standing in the kitchen eating fish fingers in his own. He was staring out at the now heavily falling rain. 'Can I come round to you, Anna? To play? I mean music. We're going back to America tomorrow.'

'Where's your grandmother?'

Anna turned to ice when she saw the gold and crimson vestments gleaming around the Aga, a mitre contracting on one hotplate and Dulcie's funeral hat on the other.

'They put her back in bed, I think.'

'And you didn't even go up to *see,*' said Anna. 'What rubbish you are, Herman.'

*

35

Dulcie was sitting up in bed, her hair fallen into extraordinary Napoleonic corkscrews, her eyes immense, and downing a double Famous Grouse. 'He's gone,' she said. 'He didn't say goodbye.' She wept.

'Who?' Anna took her in her arms and rocked her.

'No need for that,' said Dulcie. 'Fiscal-Smith, of course. I've known him over sixty years. My oldest living friend. I can't believe it. I am *mortified*.'

'But Dulcie, you didn't want him. You didn't invite him. He drives you mad. And to be truthful, you deserve better. Dulcie?'

'Yes. Well, no. You see, he's never been *known* to leave anywhere early, unless, of course, he's been kicked out. I'm afraid that *does* happen. He was never exactly one of us. Not important to us. We didn't know much about him. Though I believe that somehow Veneering did. Somewhere long ago. I never wanted to be close to him, he was so boring. But you see, this morning I was locked in the church with him. We had to wrap ourselves up together in the golden cope.'

'Oh, Dulcie! He'll get over it. He's used to being ignored.'

'Oh, the vestments!'

'Dulcie, I'll see to them. Now get up, I'll find you some clothes and you can come over to us. I've sent Herman over already. I'll make the kids cook the lunch. Where's your daughter?'

'Susan's driving him to the station.' Dulcie began to cry again. 'He's so ashamed. He was always frightened of being shamed. It's the Yorkshire accent. And – he never said goodbye.'

'Come on. Get this jersey on.'

'He won't come back. He's a terrible bore. I don't like him, but Willy said he was a very good lawyer. Incorruptible.'

'Like Veneering, then?'

'No,' she said, her mind at last at work. 'No. Not like Veneering. Simpler than Veneering. But he's the last link. The last friend.'

'Coat,' said Anna. 'Gloves. Headscarf, it's still raining. Put your feet in these boots.'

As Anna's car – Dulcie in the headscarf seated beside her, hardly up to her shoulder – passed Old Filth's house in the dell, Anna looked down at its front door and saw a window slightly open. The five-barred gate was padlocked but behind it something queer and very large had appeared, wrapped in a tarpaulin. There came a sudden insolent puff of smoke from Old Filth's medieval chimney.

Better say nothing, thought Anna. Enough for one day. And it's still only nine o'clock in the morning.

Chapter Seven

Susan, clamp-jawed, had not looked towards Old Filth's house as she took Fiscal-Smith to the station and nor did she, alone, on the way back. She was taken up with thoughts about her mother, who was obviously going downhill fast. Not fit to be left alone. Anna's a godsend, but you can't expect . . .

And Herman and I go back to America tomorrow. I wonder when I ought to tell her that I'm not married any more? Herman hasn't told her. Well, I *can't* tell her. It would be all over the village.

And as to what she's done *now*! Not so much this senile episode in the church. It's what she's done to poor little Fiscal-Smith. She's bloody hurt him. She *can* hurt. She does. She used to hurt poor old Dad but she doesn't remember. He had to find new books to read all the time and work for the Thomas Hardy Society, which got him only as far as Dorchester. He asked me to look after her but she's so silly. He knew she was silly. I don't think he ever spotted that she's also rather *nasty*. Got me from under her feet in Hong Kong as soon as I was out of the pram. Off to a boarding school in England – her old school, of course. I hated Hong Kong. I hate all that last lot who came Home, with their permed hair, thinking they were like the last debutantes curtseying in the court of heaven. Hate, hate, hate ...

'My mother,' she told the passing trees along the lanes towards St Ague, 'let everyone call me Sulky Sue from the beginning. I guess she was the one who invented it. She's hard, my mother. She's not altogether the fool she makes herself out to be: the fool who is very sweet. She's neither foolish nor sweet, really. She's manipulative, cunning and works at seeming thick as a brick. And *nasty*.'

Through tears, on Privilege Hill Susan braked as a woman passed in front of the car. It was the tall, incredibly old woman who was at the do in London yesterday. In pink. Silk. Long coat. She's still in it! It's Isobel. She's got Betty Feathers' pink umbrella. Of course, Isobel.

Lovely-looking person. Wish she was my mother.

At least there's plenty of money. Dulcie will never be a burden to me. But we must think about death duties one day soon. She won't like it, but we must.

And Fiscal-Smith. Ancient little Fiscal-Smith. Ma's really hurt him this time. Deeply twisted in the knife. Whatever has she said to him? Oh God – I wish I had a mother I could love. I wonder if she's beginning to like him, or something.

I must go and see Anna to say goodbye.

PART TWO:
TEESSIDE

Chapter Eight

Florrie Benson – that's to say she was Florrie Benson before she married the man from Odessa in Herringfleet, Teesside, England, ten years back in 1927, and became Florrie Venetski or Venski or some such name – Florrie Benson walked every day of the school term with her son to see him on the school train.

The son was ten, the place the cold north-east coast of England, the time 7.30 in the morning and the year 1937.

The boy, Terence, did not walk beside her. He never had, from being five. He disappeared ahead of her the minute they were over the front doorstep.

It was not that he was in any way ashamed of being seen with his mother. He never had been. It was just that life was an urgent affair of haste and action and nothing in it should be missed.

He was a big, fair, good-looking, lanky, athletic sort of child, in top gear from the start, his mother plodding behind him. By the time she had caught up with him on the station platform he had disappeared into the raucous mob of local children, his flash of white-blond hair running among them like a light.

Florrie never even turned her head to look for him. Never had. She arranged herself against the low rails by the ticket office, her kind, big hands hanging down over it, her smiling brown eyes gazing at the cluster of girls – always girls – who rushed to her like chickens expecting grain. All she seemed to do was smile. What the girls talked to her about goodness knows, but they never stopped until the train came.

Florrie was not particularly clean, or, rather, her clothes were rusty and gave her skin a dark tint. Sometimes the schoolgirls, daughters of steelworkers and not very clean either, stroked her arms and hands and offered her sweets which sometimes she accepted.

Florrie didn't fit in. Her essence seemed to be far away somewhere, way beyond her stocky figure. She suggested another life, a secret civilisation. She looked a solitary. For her ever to have shouted out towards the boy, Terence, to remind him of something would have been almost an insult to both, but an invisible string seemed to run between them.

Terence – Terry – the spark running in the wheat – never looked at his mother as he ran in the crowd, never waved goodbye when the train came in. When the children had been subsumed into it and it had steamed away on its six-mile jour- ney along the coast, Florrie would heave herself off the railings, nod towards the ticket office ('Now then, Florrie? 'Ow are yer?') and make for home. Her daily ritual was as much a part of local life – quite unexplained – as the train itself, its steam and flames, the fireman shovelling in the coal with the face and muscles of Vulcan. She never seemed to watch him but he was not unaware of her. He sweated in the red glow and wiped his face with a rag.

No other mother came to the station. When the children

44

were smaller the other mothers used to shout: ''Ere, Florrie. Can you look to him?' Or her. Very occasionally at the beginning Florrie would find herself near one or other, licking a handkerchief and scrubbing at a face, straightening the slippery scrap of a tiny green and yellow rayon tie. Never Terry's.

Every morning, then, for five years Florrie would heave herself off the railing and back down the road again to number 9 Muriel Street, so close she could have waved him off at the front door. And from the very start he'd got home again from the station alone. He crossed over the iron footbridge out of the alley and into some bushes. Everyone, including Florrie, seemed vague about the home train's time of arrival, and as he got older he began to make small differentials to his front door, preferring the back door in the paved grey alley where there were sheds and a cart house and black stains of blood. The blood was ingrained into the dip around the central soakaway where for years the butcher had slaughtered a beast every Thursday morning. The back street stank of salt. Then he ran round home and in at the front.

When he grew to be eight or nine he told them at home that his day at school was longer now and he would be late, then he began to take off regularly down Station Road, past the chip shop and the corn store to the bandstand on the promenade looking towards the sea. He clambered about on the flaky iron lacework and the peeling iron pillars that supported its dainty roof. He stayed there maybe half an hour, doing somersaults on the railings, or dancing about or just staring at the grey sea. Herringfleet had once had a brass band that played airs from *The Merry Widow* or Gilbert and Sullivan to people in hats and gloves who had sat out on deckchairs on the promenade, but Terry knew nothing about that. He didn't know the meaning of 'bandstand'. He'd slide away home

45

through the back streets again and come in at the front door as if he'd just got off the train.

Inside the tiny house the scene was unchanging and he scarcely registered it. His father lay on the high bed facing the street door, beside him a commode covered with a clean cloth. An iron kettle hung from a chain over the fire, puffing and clattering its lid, and the window above the sink was misted over with steam. Occasionally, on good days, his father might be in a chair, but usually, summer and winter, the long, tense figure lay on its back, coughing and coughing and sometimes swearing in Russian 'or whatever they speak in Odessa', as Nurse Watkins down the street said. Nurse Watkins would have left a minute or so before Terry got home from school, a tray put out on the kitchen table with big white teacups with a gold trefoil on the side and a broad gold rim. There'd be a plate of bread and butter with another plate on top of it. She came in every day and was paid half a crown now and then, because the families were in some way connected. She would wash out the Odessan's long flannels in Lux flakes and put him in clean ones, rub his joints, shake the bit of sheepskin someone had once brought down from Lone Hall on the moors. It still smelled of sheep-dip. It prevented bedsores.

Nurse Watkins didn't seem to have had any training anywhere but there was nothing she didn't know. She was midwife to the town and she laid everyone out at death and she told lascivious corpse-stories. She had gypsy eyes and earrings, and had been briefly at school with Florrie but had left at twelve. Over the years she had looked long at the Odessan while he had looked only at the ceiling. She stroked back his bright hair on the pillow and shaved him with a cut-throat razor when he would allow it. Florrie did the toenails herself, but not well.

'Train late again, then?' his father said to Terry. He spoke in Russian.

'Yes. Late,' said Terry, also in Russian. 'She'll be late in, too. Winter coming. Getting dark.'

Terry made tea in the brown pot and let it stand on the hob until it was brewed.

'Is there any biscuits?' He spoke in English now. 'Why'st there's never a biscuit?' and his father roared back in Russian about his grammar.

'Dist wan' a biscuit then, Dad?'

'*Do you want*,' said his father.

'There's bread.'

Sometimes his father lifted up a hand, which meant yes.

Then Florrie would be back with them, telling Terry in broad Teesside patois where to find biscuits. (In her bag, to stop Nurse Watkins.) She would refill the kettle and swing it back over the fire for the next brew.

All three knew how tired she was.

All that day she had been unrecognisable, black as a Negro, a man's thick tweed cap pulled over her hair, back to front. A man's thick coat, made thicker by years of grime, had been tied with rope round her middle. All day she'd been perched up high on a bench across the coal cart that she kept in the alley alongside the shed of the scrawny little horse and the coal store. The butcher's men often gave her a hand getting everything together, if they were there.

Three days a week she clopped round the town on the cart through all the back streets, shouting, 'COAL' in a resounding voice. The lungs of a diva. 'Coal today,' she shouted, and from the better houses of the ironmasters in Kirkleatham Street the maids ran out in white cap and apron, twittering like starlings. 'Three bags now, Florrie,' 'Four bags,' and watched her heave

47

herself down off the dray, turn her back, claw down one sack after another with black gloves stiff as wood. She balanced the bags along into coalhouses or holes in stable yards, showering down coals and coal-dust. She took the money and dropped it inside a flat leather pouch on the rope belt around her stomach. She adored her work.

'Cuppa tea, Florrie?'

'No time, no time.'

A long slow sexy laugh, then back on the dray. Street after street. The horse knew where to stop. Trade was steady. Her call was tuneful, rather like the rag-and-bone man's, but richer. Almost a song.

Fifty years on, Sir Terence Veneering QC, drinking in the Colonial Club, Hong Kong, happened to mention to someone in the Protectorate that he had been born in Herringfleet, and was told that, before the war, there had been a Northern woman, larger than life, who had delivered coals. Or so it was said. In the poverty-stricken North-East – in the middle of the Depression.

Florrie drove the dray round to the back. She took the horse to the shed and fed it, rubbed it down and, if there was no one about to help her, she dragged the dray into the cart house. There was a communal bath-house for Muriel Street and she paid a penny to have it to herself on coal days. She poured hot water from the brick tub all over herself with a tin can. She washed her hair and feet and hands and then her body with a block of transparent green Fairy soap. Then she dried herself on a brown towel, rough as heather.

Above the crooked, unpainted doors of the cart house hung a hand-painted wooden sign in green and gold saying VENETSKI COAL MERCHANT and the exotic flourish to it was the register, the signature, the stamp of proof, of Florrie's past happiness.

The sign painter was the foreign acrobat and dancer who had arrived in the town over ten years ago with a circus troupe who put up a big top on the wasteground by the gasworks for 'ONE WEEK ONLY'. The tent had sprung up overnight like a gigantic mushroom, with none of the glitter and coat-tails of Bertram Mills but an old, threadbare thing, grey and frightening, an image from the plains of Ilium. And how it stank!

'They're called Cossacks,' said the cognoscenti of Herringfleet. 'They can dance and kick right down to their ankles with their bottoms on the floor. They shout out and yell and make bazooka music, like the Old Testament Jericho. They're Russian.'

'What they doing 'ere?'

'It's since they murdered the Tsar. They want the world to see them. It's a sort of mix of animal and angel. Russia's not a rational country.'

The man selling tickets didn't go in much for angels. Long, miserable face. He said they had killed the Tsar years ago!

But young Florrie Benson saw an angel that night. She had taken money from her mother's purse to buy a ticket for the show and was at once translated. She heard a new music, swam in a new fierce rapture. She watched the superhuman contortions of the exciting male bodies. Her skin prickled all over at their wild cries. In a way, she recognised them.

There was one dancer she couldn't take her eyes off. Her friend next to her was sniggering into a handkerchief. ('For men, it's right daft.') But the next day Florence stole more money and went to the Cossacks alone. She went every night that week, and the final night she was up beside him on the platform when he fell from a rope. She was ordering a doctor, roaring out in her lion's voice. People seemed to think she must be his woman. She never left his side.

*

49

The rest of the Cossacks melted away, and they and their tent were gone by morning in their shabby truck. Florrie, the English schoolgirl, stayed with him at the hospital and wouldn't be shifted. Doctors examined him and said his back was probably not broken but time would tell. Someone said: 'He's a foreigner. Speaks nowt but heathen stuff. He'll have to be reported.'

Yet nobody seemed to know where. Or seemed interested. The local clergyman who was on the Town Council went to see him, and then the Roman Catholic priest who tried Latin and the Cossack's lips moved. Each thought the other had reported him to the authorities, without quite knowing what these were.

'They'll be in touch any day from Russia to get him back.'

They waited.

'There was a couple of Russians died of food-poisoning last year off a ship anchored in Newcastle. Meat pies. The Russians was in touch right away for body parts. Suspected sabotage.'

But nobody seemed to want the body parts of the Cossack who lay in the cottage hospital with his eyes shut. He talked to himself in his own language and spat out all the hospital food. And only the schoolgirl beside him.

'Back's gone,' they told her. 'Snapped through. He'll never walk again.'

The following week he was found, standing straight, at the window, six foot four and looking eastward towards the dawn and the Transporter Bridge at Middlesbrough, an engineering triumph. It seemed to interest him. When the nurses screamed at him he screamed back at them and began to throw the beds about, and they couldn't get near to him with a needle. Someone called the police and somebody else ran round to find Florence.

She was taken out of school and to the hospital in a police car, no explanations; and when she was let into his isolation ward she looked every bit woman and shouted, 'You. You come 'ome wi' me. *Away*!' 'Away' is a word up there that can mean anything but it is chiefly a command.

She left her address at the hospital and commanded an ambulance. The ward sister was drinking tea and smoking a cigarette with her feet up. Florrie got him into the ambulance and out of it again by herself, half on her back. She had a bed fixed up ready. The aged parents, never bright, shook their heads and drowsed on. 'Eh, Florence! Eh, Florrie Benson – whatever next?'

The dancer stayed. He lay, staring above him now. Nobody came. Florrie went to the public library in Middlesbrough to find out about Cossacks. She came back and stood looking at his curious eyes. She imagined they were seeing great plains of snow spread out before him. Multitudinous mountains. The endless Steppe. She got out some library books and tried to show him the photographs, but they didn't seem to mean anything to him.

She gave up school. She was sixteen, anyway. Her old parents went whimpering about the house, faded, and both were dead within the year.

Florence was pregnant, and even so nobody was interested in the Cossack. Neighbours came round but she was daunting. If she had been a boy it would all have been different. Serious enquiries. But, even pregnant, nothing was done for Florence.

After a time the man began to walk again, just to the window or the door on the street. Or into the ghastly back alley.

One day Florrie came home from buying fish to find him gone.

It was for her the empty tomb. The terror and the disbelief were a revelation. She ran everywhere to look for him and, in the end, it was she – out of half the parish – who found him, on the sand dunes staring out over what was still being called (occasionally) the German Ocean. The North Sea.

She brought him limping and swearing home and, at last, being well acquainted now with the Christian cross that lay in the warm golden hair on his chest, she went to the Catholic priest, leaving Nurse Watkins in charge for two shillings and fourpence. There were very few half-crowns left now.

The priest lived in a shuttered little brick house beside his ugly church over on the breakwater. Nobody went there except the Irish navvies from the steelworks.

'Russian?' asked Father Griesepert. 'Communist, you say?'

'No. He's definitely Catholic.'

'How do you know?'

'He doesn't believe in taking precautions.'

Father Griesepert said that he would call. He said that, actually, he had already been thinking about it.

'Name?' Father Griesepert shouted.

Nobody had actually asked the Cossack's name. The Catholic priest bullied the sick man in a loud voice. He tried a bit of German (on account of his own strange name, which was one of the reasons for his isolation here).

'Address? Home address?'

The man looked scornful.

'Name of circus?'

Silence. Then 'Piccadilly' and a great laugh.

Suddenly, in English, the Cossack said, 'My name is Anton.' ('Anton,' whispered Florence, listening to it.)

'Very unlikely he's a Cossack. I'd guess he comes from Odessa,' said the priest. He rubbed his hands over his face as if he were washing it. 'This woman,' he said in loud English to the man, 'is with child.'

Anton understood.

'You must be married before the birth.'

Anton looked at Florence as if he had never seen her before.

Florence went to get the priest his whisky.

They all said prayers together then, and Griesepert named the wedding date. 'We must, of course, inform the authorities.' He was met by two pairs of staring eyes.

'You are a Catholic, Florrie Benson.' She seemed uncertain. 'Your parents were lapsed. But I remember baptising you as a child. That child has now to have her own child and it must be brought up as a Catholic. It must go to a Catholic school. You must bring it to the church. And your marriage must be preceded by a purification.'

'A *purification*, Father?'

'Have you no concept of your faith?'

'You never gave me any!'

She stretched out her rough hand in a gesture which was – for her – hesitant, towards the Cossack's hand and together they both glared at the priest. Then, between them in assorted words, from God knows where, they made a stab at the Catechism, Anton's face rigid with contempt.

Florrie's face was alight with joy. The baby in the womb stirred.

Anton tried. When Florrie was in the ninth month and couldn't walk far he began to limp about the town looking for work.

There was almost no money left by now from the wills of Florrie's parents and so he became a caretaker at the private school at the end of the town. When they found that he spoke several languages, he began to teach classes there. His English improved so quickly that it almost seemed that it had always been there, beneath the other languages. He began to meet educated people in the good houses across the park towards Linthorpe. The new great families of the ironmasters. Some of them were German Jews. In these houses he behaved with a grave, alien formality, but with a seductive gleam in his eye. It seemed that he was a gentleman. It was confusing.

Soon he was being invited to dinner – always, of course, without Florrie – by the headmaster of the private school and his artistic wife while, in Muriel Street, Florence suckled the child over the kitchen range. She sang to it, made clothes for it, wished her mother were alive to see it. Wished she had been kinder to her mother.

Her husband, seated at the headmaster, Harold Fondle's, great mahogany dining table with its lace mats and good crystal, spoke in improving English and fluent French of Plato and Descartes. His English was without accent, he looked distinguished and he appreciated the wine. When anybody broached the question of his past life or his future, or his allegiances, he would raise his glass and say, 'To England.'

He grew strong again, and after the child was weaned decided to go into business as a coal merchant. He carved and then painted the gold and green sign in the slaughterhouse alley. The butcher thought little of it. ('You don't start a business by mekkin' a paintin' of it.')

When Anton's back gave out for the second time, Florrie found him twisted, lying in the alley under a sack of coal, the thin horse munching into its nosebag.

She hauled him somehow back indoors where Nurse Watkins came and they got him up at last on the bed. The baby – the alert and happy golden baby – lay watching from his cot, which was a clothes drawer. The doctor came.

Both parents that night wept.

*

54

The next day was the day of the week when Griesepert came to them with the Sacrament. He never missed. He rolled in like a walrus, snorting down his nose. He stretched out his legs towards the fender.

Today Florrie ignored the Sacrament and sat out in the yard, letting them talk. There was whisky, and firelight in the room, and the knowing-looking baby wondered whether the grim man on the bed or the fat man over the fire mattered more. The word 'father' kept recurring. The baby seemed to listen for it. As to his mother, she was milk and warmth and safe arms, but he didn't pat and stroke her like other babies do. He seldom cried. Occasionally he gave a great crow of laughter. Nurse Watkins with her brass earrings and heavy moustache called him a cold child.

Out of earshot of others, Father Griesepert told Florrie she must sleep with the Cossack again or she would lose him. (What do you know? she thought.) 'He needs a woman. It is Russian.' (And him never gone a step beyond Scarborough! she thought. And not knowing the state of Anton's back.)

Anton had visitors, just occasionally Russian-speaking, who came and went like shadows. Or *were* they shadows? Florrie and the baby sometimes slept on a mattress out by the back door. She often lay listening to the Cossack shouting at invisible companions somewhere she would never know. In the end she told the priest, who decided it came from some terrible prison of his past and that he was talking to the dead. 'We know *nothing* here, nothing of what goes on in these places. One day we might, if we live through this next war.'

'Never another war!' she said. 'Not again.'

She tried to imagine Anton's country. She knew nothing about it but snow and golden onion-topped churches and jewels and stirring cold music and peasants starving and all so blessedly far away. She did not allow herself to imagine

Anton's life before he came to her. She would never ask. At night sometimes, to stop him swearing in his sleep in words she could only guess, she'd pull out a drawer from the press where she kept her clothes and tuck down the baby among them and a chair on either end to keep the cat off and then climb on to the high bed with Anton and wrap herself round him. Sometimes, when he opened his eyes, they were unseeing and cold. There were no endearments. The sex was ferocious, impersonal, fast. There was no sweetness in it. She didn't conceive again.

Her silent faith in the little boy never lessened. Her trust and love for him were complete. As he grew up, she asked no questions when he arrived home later and later off the school train. When he was eleven she stopped taking him to the station.

For by now Terry was wandering far beyond the chip shop and the bandstand. He was roaming over the sand dunes, down over the miles of white sand towards the estuary and the lighthouse on the South Gare. On the horizon, sometimes celestially, mockingly blue, shining between blue water and blue sky, stood the lines of foreign ships waiting for the tide to take them in to Middlesbrough Docks. Spasmodically along the sand dunes the landward sky would blaze with the flaring of the steelworks' furnaces. They blazed and died and blazed again, hung steady, faded slowly. The boy watched.

He was not a rapturous child. The crane-gantry of the blast furnaces turned delirious blue at dusk, but he was not to be a painter. He noted and considered the paintbrush flicker of flame on the top of each chimney leaning this way and then that, but he sat on his pale beach noting them and no more.

He had no idea why he was drawn to the place, the luminous but unfriendly aprons of lacy water running transparent over the sand, the waxy, crunchy black deposits of sea-wrack, slippery and thick, dotted for miles like the droppings of some amphibian. The derelict grey dunes rose up behind him, empty except for tall knives of grey grass.

There would usually be a few bait diggers at the water's edge, their feet rhythmically washed by the waves. A lost dog barking out of sight.

Sometimes one or two battered home-made sand-yachts skimmed by; only one or two people watching. No children. This was not sandcastle country. No children in this hard place were brought down to play by the sea.

But there was a single recurrent figure on the beaches. It was there mostly in winter as it began to get dark: an insect figure stopping and starting, pulling a little cart, bending, stopping, pacing, sometimes shovelling something up. Always alone.

After weeks, Terry decided it was a man and it was pushing not a cart but a baby's pram. For months he watched without much interest but then he began to look out for the man and wonder who he was.

One cold afternoon he did his usual rat-run of railway bridge to the back of Muriel Street – he now passed through the room with the bed in it – and found his father's fist stuck out of the blanket towards him grasping a ten-shilling note. The wireless crackled on about Czechoslovakia and his father's lips were trying to say something. Terry pocketed the note and said in Russian, 'D'you want tea?'

'Whisky,' said his father. 'It's for the holy father. How are you?'

'I'm well.'

'You have a good Russian accent. Are you happy?'

Terry had never been asked this, and did not know.

'I'se going down t'beach now, Da.'

'Why?'

'Don't know.'

The wireless blared out and then faded. They had been the first in Muriel Street for a wireless. It stood with a flask of blue spirit beside it. Where had the money come from?

'I'se glad I know Russian,' Terry said.

'How old are you, son?'

'Going on twelve.'

Tears trickled out over the Cossack's bony face, running diagonally from the eyes to the hollows of the neck and Terry knew that, watching, there was something he should be feeling but didn't know what. He took the money and went to the shop. Let them get on with their lives. He was getting his own.

He sat down in the dunes facing the sea and soon began to be aware that he was being watched from somewhere behind his left shoulder. Before him the white sands were empty. The sea was creeping forward. He watched the trivial, collapsing waves. The steelworks' madcap chimneys were not yet putting on their evening performance against tonight's anaemic sunset.

There was a cough above him on the high dune.

Turning round, Terry saw the insect-man in an old suit and a bowler hat. The pram hung in front of him, two wheels deep in fine sand that flowed in spreading avalanches down the slope.

'Good afternoon,' said the man. 'Peter Parable.'

Terry stared.

'Of Parable Apse,' he said. 'Parable, Apse and Apse; Solicitors and Commissioners for Oaths.'

Terry stared on.

'My name is Peter Parable, senior partner, and you I believe to be Florrie Benson's boy? I was briefly at school with your mother. I am being obliged to ask for your help.'

Terry's Russian eyes watched on.

'I am a man of principle,' said the creature. 'I am not in the least interested in children. I am not of a perverted disposition. I am able to survive without entanglements, and I ask only your immediate assistance in conducting the pram down to the harder level below this dune. Today I have attempted a different route home. It has not been a success.'

The pram was up to its axles in sand.

'When I lean with all my might,' said the tiny man, 'you may assist by tugging at the back wheels, those nearest you. And then if you could sharply – *sharply* – spring to the side, I think the vehicle might achieve the beach in an upright position and of its own volition.'

Terry sat a minute considering this new language and then plodded up the dune. He kicked the rear of the pram with a nonchalance close to insolence. Close to hatred. Bloody man.

He soon stopped kicking. He tried to heave the pram upwards in his arms. He said, 'It's not going to shift. Is't full o' lead? What you got in't?'

'Black gold,' said Parable Apse. 'Black diamonds. Tiny black – and white – pearls. Now then – again!'

After at least seven heaves Terry yelled and fell to the ground, rolled sideways and watched the pram lumbering and slithering down the slope to tip over on its side upon the beach. A heap of gravelly dirt spilled over the sand. Using his shovel as a walking-stick, Mr Parable (or Apse) toddled after it, legs far apart, and Terry sat up.

'We 'ave, I fear, a weakened axle,' said the insect-man.

'You'll 'ave to leave it 'ere,' said Terry.

'Oh, it hasn't come to that. Perhaps we should empty it completely, scatter the load with simple sand and, later, return.'

Terry regarded the heap of dirt.

'And if, boy, you would carry the broken wheel and we were to push the rest of it home, then you could take tea with me.'

Terry thought: Oh, aye? and said, 'Is't far?'

'Not at all.' The man was busy covering up the mound of black gold, scratching the last of the dirt from the pram. He snapped off the damaged wheel, handed it to the boy and fell flat on his face.

'Oh, God,' said Terry, hauling him up. ''Ere. Gis 'ere. Give over. Tek t'wheel. Where we goin'?'

They paraded over the sandy path behind the dunes, across the golf links, somehow got themselves over a wooden stile watched by a lonely yellow house with empty windows. They followed a track that put them out into a street of squat one-storey houses Terry had not seen before, the long, low street of the old fishing village built before the industries came, before the ironstone chimney and the foreign workers and the chemicals and the flames. The sandstone dwellings had midget doors and windows like houses for elves. Mr Parable Apse, Commissioner for Oaths, let them both into one of these houses, leaving the pram outside, and inside they walked down a long, low tunnel of a rabbit-warren-like passageway into a kitchen scrubbed clean. Some of Mr Parable Apse's underclothing hung airing from a contraption of ropes and wooden bars overhead. He lit a hazy, beautiful gas light on a bracket, crossed to the coal fire, flourished a poker and flung a shovelful of glittering, hard dirt, like jet, into the flames. The coal fire in the grate blazed up, hot and brilliant.

'What is't?' asked Terry.

'Sea-coal. *Washed*, of course. I wash it in a bath in my yard several times a week. Out of office hours, of course, and never on the Lord's Day. In my back yard I have a pump with clear, unbounded water that cleanses like the mercy of God. The sea-coal's what washes off the ships, you know. In the estuary. Sea-coal is a bonus. Clean and beautiful, sweet-smelling, effective and *free*. Your mother should market it.'

'She's right worn out already,' said Terry. 'She's enough t'do.'

'So I hear. But you haven't yet, my boy. I expect you are meant to leave school shortly and slave at the Works? Oh, my dear boy! Sweeping a road till the end of your life.'

'They needs the money.'

'You could begin now, working casually for me. While you are waiting. I make money. I have never had any difficulty there. We could expand across this world. Parable and Benson. In the name of the Lord, of course.'

Parable, Benson and God, thought Terry. He said again, 'They needs the money. It's full-time to the Works. And me name's Venetski.'

Apse – or Parable – was washing his hands at the shallow stone sink, drying carefully between his fingers.

'How old did you say? Ah yes. I remember the visit of the Cossacks to the gasworks, though, of course, I was unable to attend. A circus is one of the Devil's ploys. There is a rumour abroad – tell me, what did you say your name was? – that you are particularly clever. Your intelligence is above these parts. You might bring your intelligence to us. Come in with me as a lawyer. It could be arranged. It is called "doing your articles" – a ridiculous and medieval concept – but a solicitor's work is the top of the world.'

(This man's a loony!)

'And even now,' said Parable Apse, 'think of Christian commerce. Sea-coal. Coal is your family business.'

'You shut up,' said Terry. 'Stop looking down on my mother.'

'Oh, never! Never! I have known her since she was born. Since her mother put her into long drawers. I loved her.'

'My dad loves her and nowt to do wi' frills. They don't speak now, me dad and mam, but it's only because of his shame. Shame at being crippled and nobody caring. And being lost.'

'He talks to you?'

'Nay – never! We's beyond talk. We talk his language together less and less. He grabs me wrist as I pass the bed. Like a torturer but it's himself 'e's torturing.'

'Why does he do that?'

'There's always money under his fingers. Tight up in the palm. He needs whisky. The mam don't know. Nurse Watkins do. She's foreign, too. He pushes t'bottle under t'mattress. When it's empty. I seen it going home in her leather bag with the washing. T'money must come from the holy father. How do I know? He's beginning to need more and more.'

He was dizzy with revelation. Revelation even to himself. None of this had emerged as words before. Not even thoughts.

'A man comes,' said Terry. 'Mam don't know. A foreign man. Talking Russian – or summat like it. When nobody's in.' He burst into tears. 'Maybe I dream it.'

Parable Apse, having dried his coal-dusted hands on a clean tea-towel, sat down by the sea-coal fire and speared a tea-cake on the end of a brass toasting-fork. The medallion on the toasting fork was some sort of jackass or demon, or sunburst god. 'How wonderful the world is,' said Parable Apse.

The fire blazed bright and the tea-cake toasted.

'We must get him vodka,' said Parable Apse. 'It does not taint the breath. Goodbye. It is more than time you went home. Take the tea-cake with you. I will butter it. I shall expect you to relish it.'

On the doorstep Terry heard him bolting the door on the inside. They sounded like the bolts of a strong-room.

Loopy, he thought. Silly old stick.

He didn't go again to the beach that week. He wandered to the nasty little shops in the new town and the Palace Cinema. He had a bit of pocket money and went in and asked for vodka at the Lobster Inn. He was thrown out. He wanted a girl to tell this to. It surprised him. The girls at his school sniggered and didn't wash much. They hung about outside the cinema. One or two had painted their mouths bright red. You could get a tube of it at Woolworths for sixpence. They shouted to him to come join them, but he didn't stop. He dawdled home.

Chapter Nine

The headmaster of Terry's school did not live on the premises or go in daily on the train. He lived several miles inland on the moors. He was a healthy man and often pedalled into Herringfleet on a bicycle with a basket on the front stuffed full of exercise books corrected the night before, for he was a teacher as well as a headmaster.

He and the bike made for the Herringfleet beaches – he always checked the tide-tables and, dependent on the condition of the sand, he walked or rode the six miles to school, thinking deeply. He always wore a stiff white riding mac. With a broad belt and a brown felt homburg hat. Sometimes he had to walk beside his bike when the sands were soft, sometimes push it hard, but he was always very upright and to his chagrin rather overweight. There were little air-holes of brass let into the mac under the arms for ventilation. Despite his healthy, exhausting regime he was a putty-faced man who never smiled. It was rumoured that there was a sick wife somewhere. He had a son at the school who got himself there on the train like most of them, and home again by his wits. A clever, little, younger boy. Fred. Terry liked him.

On the morning beaches the headmaster (a Mr Smith) often came upon Peter Parable doing an early sea-coal stint before going to his solicitor's office. They nodded at each other, Parable's gaze on the black ripples in the sand left by the tide. Smith would briskly nod and pass by, growing smaller and smaller until he was a dot disappearing up the path that led to his school assembly and the toil of the term. Smith and Parable had been at the school together as boys but hadn't cared much for each other. They had only their cleverness in common. Now they never talked.

That summer Parable began to watch Smith's straight back diminishing away from him. He noted the little eyelet holes of the mac, and the plumpness and the rather desperate marching rhythm. Even if he was on the bike Mr Smith always looked tired.

Better hurry up, thought Parable.

Smith, who knew that he was being watched, also knew that at some point he was going to be asked for something.

One beautiful, still morning Parable shouted out, 'Smith!'

Smith stopped the bike and placed both feet on the sand but didn't turn his head. 'What is it, man? Hurry up. I'll be late.'

'There's something you have to do. At once.'

'Indeed?' (What does Parable do at once or even slowly? Plays on the beach.)

'You have a boy at school who in my professional opinion – and opinions are my stock-in-trade as a lawyer – is remarkable. They're going to put him in the Works when he leaves you next year and you have to stop it. He must go to the university. He already verges on the phenomenal. I've begun to play chess with him. We debate. He has an interesting foreign father. Rather broken up.'

'You mean Florrie Benson's boy?'

'And . . . ?'

'They need his wages. Sooner the better. It's a bad business there. She can't go on.'

'She'll try. We both know her.'

'How could they afford a school until he's university age?'

'There are scholarships. We each got one.'

'We had better parents.'

'I won't have that,' shouted Parable after him across the sand. 'You have a boy yourself who's clever. I bet he'll be spared the Works.'

An hour later, at the end of school assembly and prayers, Smith paused for a long minute before clanging the hand-bell that sent the rabble of Teesside to their classrooms. He announced that he wanted Terry Benson in his study.

Terry, in some dreamscape, was kicked awake by his neighbours and looked about him. ('What you done, Terry?' 'Only tried getting vodka for me dad.' 'What – nickin'?' 'Nah – cash.') A new respect for the already respected Terry ran down the line.

Smith surveyed the crowd of spotty children, all thin. Greyfaced. Poor. All underfed. Terry Whatsisname – Benson's white-gold hair and healthy face shone among them. (It's said she gets him tripe.)

We'll get that hair cut, Smith thought. Start at the top. I'll write to the father.

'Take a letter, Miss Thompson,' he said, back in his office.

'I'm not sure Florrie Benson can read,' said the secretary. 'Me mam said she was useless at school. And the father's a cripple and only talks Russian. He's a retired Russian spy.'

*

67

The letter was typed, nevertheless, and sat waiting for Terry to collect and take home.

At the end of the afternoon the headmaster, Smith, came in and pointed at it and said, 'Letter, Miss Thompson?'

'Oh,' she said, 'he never came. I'll tek it. I know where he lives, down Herringfleet. On my way home.'

'No,' said Smith, 'I'll drop it in. I can take the bike that way. Say nothing to the boy. He's probably been trying all day to forget it. I'll bike along the sand.'

'You tired, sir?'

'Certainly not,' he said, pulling on the ventilated mackintosh that made him paler still. 'Certainly not! Box on.'

By teatime, Florrie cooking brains and hearts on a skillet, the letter was lying across the room on the doormat. The Odessan was having a better day and was in a chair. His back was to the door, but he sensed the letter. He said, 'We have a letter. I heard a bicycle and a man cough. Pick it up, will you, Florrie?'

'No,' said Florrie adding dripping, peeling potatoes.

'Then I'll wait for Terry to do it. Where is he?'

'Mebbe it's not for you,' she said. 'T'last one was to me. And what came o' *that*?'

Years before, there had come a letter on the mat that she remembered now like excrement brought in on a shoe. It was a letter in a thick cream envelope written in an operatic hand in purple ink.

In those days the situation at number 9 Muriel Street was still an interesting mystery in Herringfleet. Most people kept themselves at a distance. People crammed together in mean streets are not always in and out of each other's houses.

The letter had been sent without a stamp and delivered *By Hand*. It said so in the top left-hand corner. The letter paper inside was the colour of pale baked custard and thick as cloth.

Dear Mrs Vet [scrawl]y, it had said, I would be so delighted if you would bring your little boy to a fireworks party – with supper, of course – on 5th November for Guy Fawkes' celebrations at The Towers. A number of local children will be coming and we hope to give them a lasting and happy experience. 5 o'clock p.m. until 8 p.m. Warm coats and mittens. Sincerely yours. Veronica Fondle.

'She has asked me to a party,' Florrie said. 'Me and Terry.' Anton watched her blush and smile and thought how young she was. How beautiful. 'With Terence,' she said. 'Our Terence. For Guy Fawkes.' She gazed at the letter. 'It's to be a supper – unless she means we tek our supper? – and at *night*!'

'What,' he asked, 'is Guy Forks?'

'He were RC, like you. We burn a model of him every year. Since hundreds o' years. Because he once tried to burn down the Parliament.'

The Odessan considered this.

'But we can't go. I haven't any clothes.'

He said, 'It just says a warm coat and mittens. You have your better coat and we can get mittens.'

'Mebbe means only the children. Their mothers will be in furs.'

'Here, in Herringfleet?' said Anton, and at once wrote the acceptance in fine copperplate on a card he found in an old prayer book. Nurse Watkins brought an envelope and took it round to The Towers, where Veronica Fondle was the head-master's wife.

*

69

On the party day Terence, then not yet four, was scrubbed, polished and groomed but then became recalcitrant and unenthusiastic. He lay on his face on the floor and drummed his feet. When his mother walked in from the bath-house where she had been dressing, he roared and hid under his father's bed, for this was a woman unknown. The lace on her hat (Nurse Watkins' cousin's) stood up around her head with black velvet ribbons enmeshed. Her cloth coat Nurse Watkins had enriched with a nest of red foxtail bundles round her throat. Beneath the chin, the vixen's face clasped the tails in its yellow teeth. Poppies swayed about round the black straw hat brim. Her shoes were Nurse Watkins' mother's brogues worn on honeymoon in Whitby before the First World War, and real leather.

'You're meant to wear the veil tight against the face, like Greta Garbo, and tied round the back with the black ribbon, Florrie,' said Nurse Watkins, shushing Terry on her knee.

'I'll not get it off.'

'You're not meant to get it off.'

'Then how does I drink the tea?'

Even Nurse Watkins didn't know this.

The veil was left to float around the poppies. Anton said suddenly, 'How beautiful you are,' and Florrie disappeared out the back.

She came back saying that Nurse Watkins was to go instead of her, and Terry kicked out at the table leg while Anton picked up the book on Kant he'd been reading which Florrie had ordered for him from the public library. All he said was, 'Go!'

So outside, over the railway bridge from Muriel Street, the gas lights inside their glass lanterns were beginning to show blue as mother and son set off hand in hand.

There was no driveway up to The Towers, just three wide, shallow steps, a big oak door with circles of wrought-iron leaves and a polished brass plate alongside saying THE TOWERS, HEADMASTER: HAROLD FONDLE M.A. OXON. A chain hung down. Florrie picked up Terry and held him tight. Terry was in the full school uniform of Nurse Watkins' nephew who went to a paying kindergarten. He had had his first haircut. As Florrie stood miserably beside the chain the child shouted, 'Me, me!' and she let him drag it down. Far inside the house came a tinny clinking.

Florrie knew that something was now about to go wrong. Terry on her shoulder – rather heavy – seemed to be transfixed with terror by both the sound of the bell and the poppies in the hat. She set him down and clutched his hand. When the door opened she thought she might faint. The colours and heat within, the noise and laughter, the smell of rich food and spiced fruit and sweet drinks, the rasping whiff of gunpowder, the snap of crackers, the squealing of children running madly, waving sparkling, spitting lighted things into each other's faces. The girls were all in heavy jerseys and gaiters with but-toned boots, the boys in corduroy and mufflers. Several wore the tartan kilt. Across the entrance hall, propped against a carved fireplace, leaned a huge stuffed man with a grinning mask for a face and straw tufts coming out of his ears. He was waiting to be burned.

The maid who had answered the door however was only Bessie Bell, the gypsy girl who'd known Florrie since child-hood.

'Eh, Florrie!' she said. ''Ere. I'll tek Terry in.'

'I'll tek 'im in meself, Bessie.'

'No, it's just to be 'im,' said Bessie. 'She said.'

'*Marvellous*,' cried a large woman, wearing a musquash coat, square-shouldered, bearing down on them in the porch.

'You found your way then, Mrs Van – Van Erskine? *Splendid*. We are short of *boys*.'

Behind the woman a door stood open upon a glittering dining room, a gleam of white cloth and shiny glasses. Silver cakestands. Three-tiered, laden plates.

Then Florrie was out again on the steps alone.

She wondered if she was meant to sit there until it was eight o'clock. Three hours. It was quite dark already. And cold.

She wasn't going home, though. *Oh* no! Nurse Watkins must never know. But there was nobody she knew round here to call in on. Especially dressed like this. There was the refreshment room over the station, but the sandwiches were all curled up under glass and anyway she'd no money. And it might be closed. Father Griesepert? His church down by the beach would be locked up. It was a creepy place anyway. In the Presbytery he'd be drowsing now all by him-self, alone with his whisky and his thoughts about purity. She'd never gone to him – nor he to her – when her parents were dying.

The mist was thickening outside the ironwork porch of The Towers and she longed suddenly for her parents. Her father had once been a powerful, forceful, political man. Oh, she wanted a man! A man who stood straight and strong, who'd have brought the child here instead of her and looked round to see if the place was good enough. She folded herself down on the top step and began to disentangle the veil from the vixen's teeth.

She wondered what Terry was doing.

If he needed the you-know-what, would he ask?

He still had to be helped with buttons. He'd not long fin-ished with the chamber pot. She often went with him down the privy in the yard, especially in the dark. All those other children! Shouting and dancing about with the flaming wires. They were all so much older. Why ever had Terry been invited?

He wouldn't be crying though. Terry never cried.

But, well, he might just be. He might be crying now. Would they notice him? Would they any of them have the gump to think he might never before have been out in the dark? Would they look after him around the bonfire? Would he scream when he saw the man burning? Would they care?

That wild Bessie! No help there. And Florrie'd seen other people. All the proud horse-faced nannies in that hall. Eyebrows raised. She'd known Anton was wrong about the kids all being in uniform. Maybe in his country. Not here. Except if it was a sailor suit, and wherever would she get a sailor suit? Terry's not a princeling.

They might be being unkind and laughing at him. At this moment he might be screaming with fear. She'd seen his face as they grabbed him and carried him away. They all said he was advanced. Very, very, very clever. But she'd seen his solemn face ...

He thinks I've left him and that he won't see me again. Fear blazed to inferno and she scrambled from the step through a laurel border and round to the back of the house to its rows of lighted windows and doors and the waiting bonfire. She stepped into a flowerbed and looked into a long room full of children sitting round a banquet.

It was a Christmas card of pink and gold and scattered with glitter. There were cartwheels of cakes, pyramids of sweets and fruit. Nannies in dark blue dresses stood behind almost every child's chair, talking to each other out of the sides of their mouths but never taking their eyes off their charges. Iron-masters' children. The other side of the tracks. She couldn't see Terry.

One nanny was pressing a rather torpid child into a high-chair facing Florence. All the children were being firmly controlled.

They'll not forget the rules, these ones, she thought. There'll be no fight left in them.

She knew that this stuff wasn't for Terry. Where was he?

She sensed an event. A few children were being restrained from banging spoons on the tablecloth and a tall iced cake was being carried in by a heavy smiling man who gripped a pipe between his teeth. Mr Harold Fondle, MA, Oxon! A maid came and began to cut the cake. Where, where was Terry?

Then she saw him. He was so close to her that she could have stretched to touch him but for the glass in the long window. He had his back to her. With his newly cut hair he looked like a tiny man. In both hands he held a glass of orange juice.

He was drinking from it. He was lifting it up in the air. He was bending backwards. Then he slid off his chair and turned towards the window and she stepped back. And, oh, he was beginning to cry!

And there was blood on his face and there was a jagged arc in the glass and on his hand and he was spitting out blood. He had swallowed glass!

She began to beat her fists against the window as first one person and then another noticed that there was a crisis. Shouting and consternation surged among the nannies. One gave Terry a savage shake and glass shot across the room. Terry stopped crying and grinned and Mrs Veronica Fondle came swanning up like a barge at sunset.

Through the window Florrie heard her peahen cry: 'All well. All well, the child is probably only used to mugs.'

But Florrie was by now at the front door again, hanging on

74

the bell chain, dragging it up and down, and when Bessie answered she was across the hall and into the dining room to see Terry composedly eating porridge which some plumed assistant was spooning into him. Mrs Fondle in her furs stood near by, en route to the garden where the bonfire was being lit. Smoke and one crackling flame. 'Oh! Aha! Oh – Mrs *Verminsky*!' (She was laughing.) 'He took a *bite* from a *glass*! But *please* don't worry. Nanny has counted all the bits and we have most of them. Boys tend to do this more than girls. We give them *porridge* just in case. Wonderful in the intestines—'

Florrie seized the child in her arms as his mouth opened for more porridge. He looked at his mother and began to cry again.

'There are worse things we have to face than glass.' Mr Harold Fondle strode by, his arms spiky with rockets, towards the bonfire.

'Well, he's coming home with me now,' said Florrie. 'I've had enough.'

'But however did she *know*?' Veronica Fondle called across to her husband that night in their avant-garde twin-bedded room. Outside, the bonfire was doused and ashy, the straw man a few fragments of rags and dust. 'She must have been watching through the window. Crept into the garden. Peeping in at us!'

'Perhaps we should have invited her into the party,' said Fondle. 'He's very young.'

'Oh, I think not. There are limits.'

'I have my reasons, you know, for keeping an eye on that boy. He could become one of my stars.'

'So you say. Look, he's perfectly all right. He'd eaten an enormous tea before that orange juice. He wasn't worried when his mother came barging in.'

'Well, his mother was. Very worried.'

They laughed as they turned off their individual bedside lights, like people in a dance routine. Click, then click.

'Oh, and darling,' she said in the dark. 'The *hat*!'

'Do you know,' he said from the other bed, 'I thought the hat was rather fine.'

PART THREE:
LAST FRIENDS

Chapter Ten

When Fiscal-Smith's train reached Waterloo after the dreadful morning in Dorset, he found himself reluctant for some reason to continue his journey to King's Cross and then on to the North.

He was, for one thing, not exactly expected at home. He had intimated that he had been invited to stay for some time with old friends. And also, he was now feeling distinctly unwell.

Already it had been a long morning for a man of his advanced years: up at 5 a.m. in the Dorset rain to examine a building half a mile away, said to be burnt out and which had turned out to be in perfect condition. Then that idiocy with Dulcie, locked alone with her inside the parish church and having to ring the bells for rescue. And so on.

And then Dulcie herself. Distinctly unwelcoming. And the awful daughter. And the glaring grandson.

Sometimes, he thought, one should take a long, hard look at old friends. Like old clothes in a cupboard, there comes the moment to examine for moth. Perhaps throw them out and forget them. Yes.

But he had been able to make his mark with the delightful new village family who had bought Veneering's pile, his frightful Gormenghast on the hill. Fiscal-Smith would rather like to keep his oar in there. He would be pleased to have an open invitation to sleep in Veneering's old house, tell these new people about their predecessor. Though maybe not everything about him.

Not that Veneering himself had ever once invited him there. Not even after that ridiculous lunch of Dulcie's years ago, where all the guests were senile except himself and that boy and that desolate carer. Like lunch in a care home. Turned out in the rain. Had had to walk to the station on that occasion. Walk! Couldn't do it now. Taxi would have cost three pounds even then. God knows how much now.

But there wouldn't be much chance of making his mark with the new people either. Very casual manners, these days. And Dulcie had taken against him. She'd always been a funny fish. Probably never see her again. Probably never see any of them again. Oh, well. End of it all.

At Waterloo he burrowed for his old man's bus pass and stood for a bus that crossed the bridge and turned towards the Temple. Taxi fares prohibitive and the drivers not pleasant any more. Mostly Polish immigrants. Very haughty. One had told him lately how the Poles had saved us in the war and then added, 'Now we're saving you for the second time. We *work*.' He had not replied. For the second day running Fiscal-Smith made for the Strand and the Inns of Court.

Only twenty-four hours since the bell was tolling for Old Filth.

Different scene now. Earlier in the day.

Streams of black gowns pouring about, papers flapping, laptops gleaming, wigs on rakish, neck-bands flopping in the breeze. Home, he thought, I am home and young again. Bugger Dorset and the living dead.

And it's lunchtime. I'll go to lunch at the Inn. They'll remember me. It can't be more than ten years. Say fifteen. And it's free. I am a life member – a Bencher – of this Inn.

Inner Temple Hall was roaring as he used his old key to let himself in (watch-chain). Then up the stairs. He pushed at the swing doors to the Hall. Hundreds of them inside, hundreds! Yelling! How much bigger they all are than we were. No rationing now. What a size, some of them – sitting down to plates of what looks like excellent hot food. Stacks of it. Fiscal-Smith had not been offered breakfast. Only that watery tea.

Fiscal-Smith set down his substantial overnight valise and went to pee. No gentleman now, he thought, ever makes use of the facilities on British Rail. So sad. There were once towels, even in third class. The WCs now look like oil-drums. They can trap you inside them. Enough of that for one day.

Fiscal-Smith tidied himself up and made for the dining hall, and was stopped on the threshold.

'Yes, sir? May we help?'

'Fiscal-Smith.'

'Are you a member of this Inn, sir?'

He tried a withering look.

'Bencher. For more than half a century. I am from the North. I am seldom here.'

'We may have to ask you to pay, sir.'

As he turned the colour of damson jam, someone called to him from High Table where senior silks and judges were leaning about like a da Vinci frieze. Sharks, whales, porpoises above the ocean floor. Scarcely registering the shoals of minnows in the waters below but not near them.

'Fiscal-Smith! Good God! Over here, over here. Excellent!'
And he felt at once much better.

'Been staying with old Pastry Willy's widow in Dorset.
Invited me back after Filth's do yesterday. Very old friends, of
course.'

Nobody seemed to have heard of Pastry Willy.

'Good do, I thought,' said the oldest of the great fish.
'Touching. Very well attended, considering his age. Weren't
you a particular friend?'

Fiscal-Smith sat down, comforted. Roast pork, vegetables
with nuts in, gravy and apple sauce were put before him and
he was asked if he would like a glass of wine.

'Extraordinary,' he told a childish-looking silk beside
him. 'When I was starting out and we came to lunch here it
was bread and cheese and soup and beer. And free. We were
thinner, too. And more awake, perhaps, in court in the after-
noons.'

'During the war?'

'Afterwards. Just after. Place here all dust, you know. Direct
hit. First made me think there might be a future in Building
Contracts. Early in the war I don't think there was any lunch
at all. But I was still at school then.'

'Really? Were you? Where were you?'

'Oh, in the North. I'm Catholic, you know. Roman
Catholic.'

'Not much in the way of work in those days, I hear?'

'No. Not for years after the war,' said Fiscal-Smith.
'Fighting was passé. We'd lost the taste for it. So poor we
washed our shirts and bands ourselves. Fourpence at the laundry. We bought this new stuff – detergent. "Dreft", it was
called. And Dolly Blue. Starched them too. Too poor for
wives. Tramped the streets in our demob suits looking for
Chambers.'

'It's said that even Filth and Veneering couldn't get Chambers. Did they hate each other from the start? Did you know them then?'

'I knew Veneering from being eight years old.'

'Yet nobody ever *really* knew him – we understand?'

Fiscal-Smith kept a conceited silence.

At length he said, 'I was Veneering's oldest friend on earth.'

Then he added, seeing a suggestion of Veneering's sour old-man's face somewhere up in the repaired rafters of the Great Hall, 'He was much cleverer than I was, of course. So was old Feathers – they called him Old Filth. Both wonderful brains.'

'So,' someone eating apple crumble and custard called from down the table, 'so we understand. One wonders why they stuck so long with the Construction Law. Charismatic, well educated, intellectuals. Double Firsts. A lifetime writing building contracts and a twilight of editing *Hudson*. No politics. No crime. No international highlights.'

'I can tell you why.' Fiscal-Smith stretched his short – very old – legs under the table, legs that earlier that day had been disguised under a choirboy's cassock. 'I was present. They made a joint decision. It occurred in the Brighton County Court. I was Veneering's unpaid pupil and I'd gone down with him there to observe. It was a Gross Indecency case.'

'Yes,' said the apple-crumble eater. 'Can't see Old Filth distinguishing himself there. Veneering, possibly. More worldly man. And merrier. Bit of a clown.'

'None of us was merry that day,' said Fiscal-Smith. 'All of us fairly depressed. We went to Brighton of course by train – none of us had a car. Train called the *Brighton Belle*. Beautiful train. Ran every hour on the hour. Pink linen tablecloths and table lamps even in the second class, which I think was still called third. What the first class was like – maybe solid silver and bits of parsley on the sandwiches – I don't know. Veneering and I sat at one table and aristocratic Filth sat as far away as possible from both of us at another, with his back to us, fountain pen poised. Small glass of dry sherry. Filth and Veneering hadn't then exactly quarrelled. It was long before the infidelity. Long before Filth marrying Betty. It was just something brewing. Inexplicable. Witch's brew. Or simple distaste.'

'Ah, it happens,' said the apple-crumble eater.

'Well, the train was late. Stood still God knows how long. Fizzing steam. Could hear people cough. No information, of course. No tannoys then. We stuck on the line for an hour, took two separate taxis to the Brighton County Court from the station, arrived after midday. Furious judge. Sent us to the back of the queue. Didn't get on till after three o'clock. Filth prosecuting, Veneering for the defence.'

'Gross Indecency?'

'Yes. Ridiculous. Occurred in a circus.'

'What, with animals? Bestiality?'

'No. Lion tamer's apprentice.'

'You're not making this up, Fiscal-Smith?'

'No. Lump of a lad. Retarded. Maybe Down's syndrome. Employed most of his time shovelling dung. Dirty-looking child. He'd been going round during the performances under the tiers of seats in the big top, and tickling the private parts of women in the audience with a long straw. Up through the slats.'

'You *are* making this up!'

'No. Tickle-tickle. They would all start wriggling and scratching. All round the tiers like a Mexican wave. In those days, you know, ladies' tights hadn't been invented. (Yes, thank you. I will. The claret is still excellent.) There were all these pale pink arcs of skin between the stocking-tops and the knickers. Schoolgirls, I believe, used to call the gaps "smiles" or "sights".

'Well, the lion tamer's boy went along beneath the rows tickling all the "smiles", and you should have heard the pristine Filth going on about him. "Obscene, depraved", etc. And the judge nodding his head. Veneering and I wriggling about, at first trying not to laugh. Shaking the papers about. "Perverted." Then Veneering just slammed down the brief and walked out.'

'What! Out of court? He walked out of *court*!'

'Yes. Slam, bang up the aisle, through the swing doors and out. Filth had risen to his feet, turned and watched him go. Closed his eyes as if the King had died. And nobody said a word.

'So, I thought I'd better go and find him. I asked for permission ... Judge said nothing. Looked struck by lightning. "Unheard of, unbelievable, taken ill?" etc. whispered around. I bowed, and then ran out and found Veneering dragging on a cigarette in the corridor. I said – and by the way, Filth's solicitor, the dwarf, had appeared from somewhere—'

'Yes. He is dodgy ...'

'Veneering was shouting, "Bloody pompous fucking toffs. Never been in the real world." I happened to know that Veneering had a penchant for circuses, and he thundered back into court – no excuses – and put up a great performance about what fools we were making of ourselves. Wastage of court's time. Harmless prank. Bleak life in the circus. Boy orphaned. Neglected. Confused. Unloved. Half-starved.

'But that boy got three months. *Three months!* Filth standing there, Holy Moses. Very pleased with himself. And we all paraded out except for the lion tamer's boy who was taken to the Black Maria in handcuffs.'

'No! *How* long ago, did you say?'

'Well – ages ago. Look it up. It's in the statute book. Just after the war.'

'I suppose a century earlier it would have been a hanging.'

'A century earlier,' Fiscal-Smith said, 'it would not have come to court at all. Audience would have dealt with it on site.'

'Thrown him to the lions,' said the apple-crumble lord.

'Well, anyway – this is an excellent cheese – on the way home Veneering said to me – we'd treated ourselves to a gin and orange – "That's settled it, Fiscal-Smith. I don't think I've much of a future in Crime. I'm going for the Commercial Bar." I told him that he'd probably find Old Filth there too. Filth may have won but he was way out of his depth with circuses. And easily shocked. Veneering said, "Well, I suppose that will have to be endured."'

After the coffee, Fiscal-Smith, feeling greatly restored, made for the London Underground. Yet as the tube rattled along to King's Cross, everybody sitting blank and dreary, staring at their thoughts, his good humour ebbed. It was now mid-afternoon.

In the *Flying Scotsman*, heading North – not the old patrician *Flying Scotsman* but a flashy Lowlander calling itself so – the seats, his being one of the last free, were lumpy and small. The train was cold. In two other seats at the small table for four there were two laptops plugged in and hard at work. In the fourth seat was an unwashed young man rhythmically nodding his head, an intrusive metallic hissing emanating from the machinery in his ears. The journey was to take three hours, the corridor packed solid towards the buffet and a cup of tea. No drinks trolley. Where had he put his overnight case? The luggage rack was too narrow for anything but a briefcase or a coat. He was wishing for a coat. A coat on his back. He was really cold now. Actually, he was shivering.

Nobody spoke. Nobody smiled. Many coughed. Above the perpetual restless shuffling noises of the laptops, raucous, overhead bulletins about where the train was going and where it would stop and which would be the next 'station-stop' quacked out every few minutes. Ring tones shrilled, instructions shouted into mobile phones up and down the coach had one loud universal message: that their owner was expecting to be met by a car at his destination.

Met. Fiscal-Smith had made no arrangements to be met at Darlington. He was slipping. Why ever had he wasted all that time telling those old bores on the Bench about the lion tamer's apprentice of over sixty years ago? Shouldn't drink at lunchtime. Broken the lifetime rule of his profession. Long day. Those church vestments! That time with Susan on Tisbury Station telling her about Veneering. Sulky Sue. Feeling hot now. And cold. Not so young as I was. Ninety in a few years. Ye gods!

At York, many alighted but many more struggled aboard. 'You OK, chum?' asked a Jamaican who was replacing the man with the electronic ears. Still strange to see a Jamaican up North. I like Jamaicans. Good case there once. Six months' sunlight. Veneering's junior. Old Mona Hotel outside Kingston. Sunsets. Lizards. Rum and pineapple. Case about a gigantic drain. Old Princess Royal there. Could she drink gin! Wouldn't go to bed. All her ladies-in-waiting asleep on their feet. Queen Mother? Blue eyes. Blue as Lady Mountbatten's. Now *there* was a ... Should have told those babes-in-arms at the Inner Temple how the Queen Mother once came to dinner in Lincoln's Inn and beamed round and said, 'What a lot of darkies.'

I really do feel rather ill.

*

At Darlington he clambered out, the Jamaican helping with his bag, coming along the platform with him, trying to find someone to give the old guy a hand.

No one. Dark night.

He tramped the long platform, down the steps and through the tunnel of white glazed brick. Contemptuously – no, *contemporary* – with Stevenson probably. Graffiti. Strange faces in the shadows. Urine smells. On the empty taxi-rank he waited, feeling his forehead. It was on fire.

'*Where?*' asked the taxi driver twenty minutes later. 'Yarm? It's ten mile!'

'The Judges Hotel.'

'I doubt it's going to be open this time of night. It's dark.'

'I can't get to my own house tonight, it's up on the moor. On my grouse moor, actually.'

'Grouse'll have to fly you in then. I'm not risking that road up. Come on then, mister, hop in. We'll try the hanging Judges. I'll give them a bell.'

'I was ringing church bells this morning at half-past five,' Fiscal-Smith told him, and thought, I'm wandering. This day is a feverish dream. Not good. Lived too long.

But through the oak door of what had once been the very comfortable assize-court lodging for itinerant judges, a woman in disarray was coming running, shouting and waving a torch.

'Whatever time o' night d'you call this, Fred? Why di'n't yer book in? Yes, there's a bed and yes you can have the downstairs Sir Edward had, with the goldfish and the bears. Quick, you're not well. Top-and-tail wash while I find you a hot-water bottle. I'll bring you a tray to bed. At your age! Should be ashamed. A man with a good brain – except for living in that daft place up the hill. Hot milk and aspirins. No – no, whisky. You're shaking. It'll be the bird flu and stress. Doctor first thing tomorrow. I looked down the *Telegraph* list of folk at Sir Edward's memorial service and first thing I thought, "Now then, did he tek his coat?" I meant you.'

Deep in good wool blankets – none of your duvets – roasting with two hot-water bottles, fore and aft, and a tray across his stomach (ham sandwiches which he did not want), Fiscal-Smith sank into fitful sleep. Old Filth had slept in this bed. What's left of him now in the Malayan swamp? Goldfish bubbling. Terrible teddy bears. Queer massage machine for feet. Chamber pot. *Chamber pot!* Like the Cossack and Muriel Street. 'Please do not feed the fish.' 'Click here for music.' No, no. Silence in court.

Someone was switching things off. Covering him with an extra blanket. Talking about him, but just to herself. Didn't have to answer. North is a better country.

Did I really tell them about that case? The ladies' parted legs? The 'smiles'? Personally never seen such things. Wouldn't want to. Dulcie. Very long day. Poor Veneering dead on Malta! Never thought ahead. None of us.

I shall probably die now. Bugger the Temple, the Knights Templar.

What's left of them will have to come up here to mine. Do them good.

Chapter Eleven

About ten years after the Guy Fawkes party, London blazing and bombardment of cities all over the country, Terry Venetski, safe from the Works, and now one of Mr Fondle's élite, came home from school at The Towers one day to number 9 Muriel Street carrying a third letter to his parents, formally addressed and sealed.

He was taller now than either of them, broader and stronger. His hair was still extraordinary, wild and long and white-gold, and he had the same alert charm as the baby born nearly fourteen years ago, after the Russian circus came to town.

The letter said:

In view of hostilities in the South of the country and the attacks on our ports and industrial centres, I and the Governors of my school, The Towers, are asking for parents' views on its evacuation to Canada in September.

A magnificent newly built cruise-liner recently

completed in India, the City of Benares, *has generously been put at our disposal by the government, mostly for London children rendered homeless by the Blitz. There are berths for two hundred children, all of whom will travel free. There are also private passengers, trained voluntary foster-parents for the journey, and excellent fostering promised for the time in Canada, however long this may be.*

The ship is luxuriously appointed with excellent food, entertainments and comforts. The stewards are highly trained, and love children. They almost all come from the city of Benares in India. All are ready for torpedo attacks and the ship will of course be escorted by corvettes of the Royal Navy. Mrs Fondle will be accompanying us and we plan to remain in Canada for the duration of the War.

Nothing can be agreed upon unless all parents support the evacuation. <u>*We ask for an immediate reply.*</u>
Signed
HAROLD FONDLE, MA Oxon.

Terry tossed the letter upon the bed as he came in, then went out again and down to the Palace Cinema, where he met up with a waiting girl and they went into the back row, supposedly to watch Deanna Durbin in *One Hundred Men and a Girl.*

The Cossack lay on his bed. He held the letter unopened in his hand for an hour.

Later Peter Parable came in. He and the Odessan read the letter.

The Odessan said, 'This will be the end of Florrie.'

'Send her with him. I have money,' said Parable.

'She'd not leave me. And no one will take me to Canada.'

Before long Florrie arrived, warm and clean from the sandstone bath-house and drying her soft hair. She stopped and looked at them.

'What's this then?'

She took the letter, and after reading it slowly put it down again on the bed. She filled the kettle and set it to boil. She said, 'Good thing we'se somehow got that wireless in. It's terrible, you know, in London.'

'The bombers will be up here next,' said the Odessan. 'You must move in with us, Peter Parable. They'll not let you live on by the shore.'

'Aye,' said Florrie. 'You can have his room. He'd best go, Anton.'

All three, all thinking that she never spoke Anton's name in public, began to pass the letter between them.

'Fondle's running,' said Parable. 'Calls it "escorting". In luxury. He's running away.'

'Saving himself,' said Florrie, 'and her with him.'

'If he saves his boys—? His "star" boys?'

Florrie was pouring tea carefully into the trefoil cups. 'He'd best go,' she said. 'Canada's very English. A great clean amiable country and a good long way off from trouble.'

Chapter Twelve

The night before the departure to Canada of Mr Fondle's unanimously evacuating school, Terry Venetski slid out of Muriel Street and down to the rabbit-hole houses by the sand dunes to say goodbye to Mr Parable.

He was at home. The flames from the sea-coal fire could be seen far down the passage behind him, glittering and painting the walls a rosy orange.

Parable opened the door wider and said, 'Yes? I have been waiting.'

'I couldn't come before. There's big activity. Piles of clothes. I don't know where she finds them. I told her I'd leave her all my coupons. I shan't need them in Canada.'

'Who knows?'

'She doesn't. Dad's come up with things, too. Things we never knew. There's a crucifix and a missile.'

'It will be a missal. A prayer book. Come in. I'd have thought that would have been for the holy father to give you.'

'He's given me a bobbly thing. A rosary.'

'You know my feelings about the Roman Catholic Church.

Well, I suppose you've come to see what I am going to give you?'

'It never entered my head, Mr Apse.'

'Just as well. I am giving you nothing. Nothing for the moment, that's to say, except naturally my prayers. Nothing extra for now, but there will be something in the years to come. It will be handled by my head office – you may have heard that I have branches in other parts of the country? I am speaking of my will.'

'Thank you very much, Mr Apse.'

'Parable – Peter Parable. It will not be a fortune. You must make your own: as I had to do in London on—'

'Yes, you told me that too, Mr Parable. On ten shillings a week.'

'Did me no harm. But all this is for after the war. When you are back home again. You will come back. We will win the war. But I think you should not come back up here. Go to London, where I have significant connections, which will quietly endure. You will not want.'

'I'll write, Mr Apse. From Canada.'

'Remember your Bible, boy. And I shall need to know your address before I die.'

'But, if you die, Mr Apse . . . ?'

'In order for my executors to send you your inheritance. I don't mind telling you that, chiefly on account of my esteem for your dear mother and my admiration for your father's courage, I intend to leave you twenty-five pounds.'

'Will that be per annum, Mr Ap – Mr Parable?'

'No, it will be net, boy. Your capital.'

'Why are you doing this, Mr Apse?'

'Don't grin, boy. Do not mock. I do this wholly for your mother, fool though she was not to marry me.'

*

'Did you nearly marry Mr Parable, Ma?'

'Peter Parable? I did not.'

There was a roar from the bed.

'More fool me,' she said, stirring the pot.

'No,' said Terry, and from the bed came a more acquiescent rumble. 'It wouldn't have done, Ma.'

'Well, I suppose I might have had silk stockings and a fur coat by now if I had.'

'More like,' said Terry, 'you'd have been singing hymns on the sands in a bonnet,' and the three of them laughed.

'And you'd not have had me,' said the child.

'Well, that could have been a relief.' She ladled out dumplings and rabbit stew. Then there was apple tart and custard.

'You'll miss this in Canada,' she said. 'It'll be plain stuff there.'

'Bed then, aye? Sleep well,' she said later.

His bag for tomorrow by the door. His papers in a satchel near by. 'Up early now,' she said. They did not kiss.

The Odessan took Terry's hand as he passed the bed. He put money in the hand and spoke to him in Russian. Then the Odessan roared out a spate of some other language in a new, horrible, terrifying voice and his eyes looked blind. Florrie ran out to the yard. Terry stood like an object. He said nothing. The Odessan said, 'You have Russian blood; say something, for the love of Christ. I have nothing to give you. Nothing.'

'Yes. A chess set. Make me a chess set, my da.'

'You will write or cable? Every day, my boy?'

'Of course.'

'We cannot speak directly of the love of God,' said the Odessan, 'but I can bless you.'

'Ta, Da.'

*

The next morning there was the holy father in the house. There was bustle. Sleeplessness had ceased with dawn and now they were all bemused by late heavy slumber. 'Come on, we go,' said Griesepert, and Terry found himself out on Muriel Street where Florrie said, 'Goodbye then. I'll not come to the train. Did years of that. I'll go get your da his breakfast.'

He walked with the priest to the end of the road and turned to wave, but she had gone.

On the station all Mr Fondle's evacuees were gathered just as if it were an ordinary schoolday of years ago. Today however they were going the opposite way.

There did not seem to be very many evacuees. The parents – quite a small group – stood together in a clump talking to each other rather than to their children. Most parents were being very bright. Most children seemed very young. They coursed about the platform being aeroplanes, bright and smiling, noisy and wild. Some swung their gas-masks round their heads. The gas-masks were on long shoulder-strings and in square cardboard boxes. Even Mrs Fondle carried a gas-mask, but it was boxed in black satin and on a ribbon.

'You can throw them all in the sea the minute we're out of sight of land,' Mr Fondle called, and Mrs Fondle marched about, smiling.

The tearful officials in the ticket office were crammed up against the glass partition, some with handkerchiefs against their faces. A few of the better-dressed parents gathered closely around the headmaster and his wife and the tall handsome boy (Is it Terry? they can't be sending *Terry*!) so much older than the rest.

'Is he your son?' a woman asked Griesepert. Two tiny girls in smocking dresses and Start-Rite London sandals stood silently beside her. 'He's surely too old to be an evacuee?'

'I am a Catholic priest. He is not mine.'

'Oh – the poor boy must be an orphan.' The woman waggled a finger at Terry. 'And *so* good-looking. You'll be an American Hollywood star one day.'

'We're going to Canada,' said Terry. 'Do your children know?'

'Oh, it's about the same thing,' she said.

'This boy's parents are both living. He means everything to them.'

Terry was examining the chocolate slot-machine, empty since sweet-rationing, with its metal drawer hanging out. The priest watched, hoping that Terry had heard.

Terry was still dazed and unnerved by Florrie's absence.

She'd stood at the door steady and confident as a sergeant-major. Hand on latch had said, 'Well now. Got everything then? Got t'cake? Stamps? You'll be needing a stamp when you writes home tonight from Liverpool.'

She – and Terry – knew that he would never say, 'Aren't you coming as far as the train?' That she would never kiss him in front of anybody.

He had moved his feet on the step, looking to each side of her, marking time. The shadow of his father crawling back to the bed, skirting the chamber pot, moved behind her. After a minute his father's pointed knees rose like Alps inside the snowy counterpane.

'You got one of them socks going to sleep inside one of them shoes,' said Florrie. 'That won't suit Canada. It's a good fault though, too big. No doubt they'll wash 'em in too-hot water. It's good to see you in long trousers. I'll send a second pair. Now, you remember to write *tonight*. And watch your manners.'

That was when she had gone in and shut the door behind her.

*

When the train steamed in, it gathered the children into itself, the parents flustering, faces against windows. Few children cried. Some looked unconcerned, and remote, blank as the dead. Some of the parents on the platform tried to wave little paper flags.

Inside their carriage, the Fondles were talkative and encouraging. With their entourage, they set off across the world to safety.

Terry had a corner seat in the Fondles' first-class carriage but, as the train gathered speed, he stood up, opened the window by its leather strap and leaned forward to push his head out into the blowy day. At one blast he was caught into the slide and clatter of the train, the sudden, knowing hoot from the funnel. He watched the strings of coarse red council houses, the gaunt chimneys of the ironworks above them. At his back were the Cleveland Hills where Mr Smith lived with his sick wife and little Fred. Behind the chimneys, in front of Terry and invisible, rolled in the sea towards the minefields of the sand dunes and the barbed wire and Mr Parable. All his life's landscape was passing out of sight. Here was the long fence at the end of the grounds of Mr Fondle's school. There was a FOR SALE notice up, facing the train, beside the empty fives court.

Pressed up against this fence, arms outstretched before her towards the running train, mouth gaping, face yearning, eyes blank and terrible and blind, stood his mother.

Then the train had swished and trundled by and Terry stood at the window until Veronica Fondle twitched at his coat and told him to close it and sit down.

He never knew if his mother had seen him passionately waving.

Chapter Thirteen

A mile or two inland and over sixty years later, old Fred
Fiscal-Smith was deep in some gleaming, bubbling ocean.
Seaweed trailed in it and there were soft, gulping bubbles,
tropical ripples and gentle waves. Java, perhaps? Wonderful
case there in the seventies. Faulty refrigeration plant, junior to
Veneering. And to Filth.

But Fiscal-Smith's forehead seemed to be resting now on a
smooth glass, globular surface, and he was a baby again.
More alarmingly, he was gazing into a wide mouth with bright
lips turned inside-out like a glove, opening and shutting,
moving tirelessly, eyes staring with disbelief. Ye gods, it was a
goldfish, and he was slipping off the edge of the bed!

Where'd she gone? The madame?

A bang and a rushing figure, and she was back. It was
morning in the best bedroom of the Judges Hotel and the curtains were being drawn back. Her voice rattled on. And on.

'Now then, Fred. Thermometer. Straighten yourself out.
We'll be gathering up them goldfish off the floor. They's meant
to soothe the guests, not frighten them. My own idea. Copied

from dentists. It's raining and right cold – and almost afternoon. You've slept twelve hours, Fred. You'll be right in a day or two. You'd best stay here till you is.'

'No, no. I must get home.'

'I've told him, your so-called "ghillie", I call him Bertie as I call you Fred, Fred, when we're alone. Since Herringfleet School—'

'Tell Bertie—'

'I've told him. Returned from one of his memorial services, I said, with the flu. Staying here. Told him to bring down any post, except that, knowing him, he won't. Bone idle. Here's the paper. More about the Service. What a mob of double barrels!'

'Do go away. I'm not awake. Home . . .'

'Now don't tell me Lone Hall's ever been home, Fred. Just as Fiscal-Smith's not the name you were baptised. You and I hailed from Ada Street first, just as His High and Mightiness hailed from Muriel Street. It was your dad fancied the Hall up here long since, and now you can't get rid of it. Smith was your name.'

'I'd never try to change my name. I'm denying nothing about Ada Street. After all, I've come back up here. To the North. Might never have left Hong Kong, if I'd wanted. But I'm faithful.'

'Breakfast. Here. Eat it. They've done you eggs and bacon.'

He munched, his back against the pillows. Beside him on the table the goldfish hung in their blob of ocean, then shrugged and shimmered away into some ornamental pebbles and ferns.

'You're kind, Margaret. *You*'d never order me out. I'll stay a day or so, for old times' sake. I can't really afford . . .'

'You're worth millions, Fred. Shut up. What happened down there? Something's upset you.'

'Oh – didn't know many people. Didn't feel very welcome, as a matter of fact. Old friends change. Or die. Or both. Thinking of Hong Kong – I was Sir Edward Feathers' best man there, you know – and, well, rather aware that nobody has ever, exactly, *wanted* me. And the obituaries were full of mistakes. Terry Veneering's "childhood in Russia"! Old Filth's "uneventful life"! Ha!'

'Come on, get your own life, Fred.'

'Bit late now, Margaret. Everything's getting right dim, now.'

'You said that like a local, Fred. Go back to sleep.'

'Aye. And put a cloth over them bloody fish,' he said in a voice that would have been unrecognisable in the Temple. As he fell asleep he said, 'Remember Florrie Benson? Terrible business that. Terrible world.'

Chapter Fourteen

The many-decked cruise ship stood like a city in Liverpool Dock and the faces looking down from the upper decks were dots. Gangplanks stood robust and heavy. Rows of lifeboats, all tested and passed, hung like fruits.

There had been a last-minute delay and now the date of embarkation would be tomorrow, Friday the thirteenth. Normally no big ship would have risked such a date, but there was a waiting group of convoy ships, and Liverpool was being heavily bombed and more bombardment expected. There was urgency.

The ship was carrying up to two hundred children, mostly the East End of London poor, homeless, and some orphaned already in the Blitz. National newspapers had been publishing photographs of dead children laid out in rows. Churchill had not yet vetoed these evacuations by sea but there was serious lobbying about patriotism and one's country being the noblest place to die; and also suggestions, since the sinking of a similar ship carrying children less than a month earlier, of nervousness.

Most of the London children had said goodbye to their

parents at Euston Station and continued by train to Liverpool, where the delay had meant a stay of two nights in rat-infested hostels. Some had cried, a few fallen ill – there was a case of chickenpox (this boy was taken home) – but most of the rest were noisy and excited and looking forward to the six days of crossing the Atlantic to a new life. None of them mentioned the partings from home. They had transformed themselves into a new, intimate community consisting only of each other.

'When are we *going*?' they lamented. Not only the German bombs at night but the huge barrage of Liverpool gunfire thundered all around them, hour after hour all night. 'Soon,' they were told, 'soon.' Two of the children had been on board the earlier evacuee ship which had been torpedoed a fortnight ago, but everyone saved. These two heavy girls seemed stolidly unconcerned.

There were also the paying passengers, 'businessmen, diplomats and professors and people of pre-war opulence', as was later reported in the press. Among these were Mr and Mrs Fondle and their party from North Yorkshire, expecting to board the *City of Benares* at once.

But the train had been slow and the Fondles had been obliged to sit with their élite group of children in one of the sheds on the quay. And, later, their supper was the same as the children's. Veronica Fondle had picked at the slices of National Wheatmeal Loaf – pale grey – a little grey pie, some wet grey cabbage and a dollop of 'instant potato' called Pom.

The Fondles did not seem to be hungry. They leaned back from the communal bench and smoked black cigarettes with gold tips. Mrs Fondle patted the seat next to her and said, 'Not long now, Terence.' The poorer children raced about and screamed and shouted like a flock of autumn starlings suddenly wheeling, like smoke, out of sight of the dormitory sheds.

Terry said, 'There's not one of them older than ten.'

'Oh, I wouldn't say that, Terry. Terry, you must stop saying "wan". You are travelling with us.'

He could think of no answer. He could not bear her face or her voice. After a time he took a last bite into the so-called tart ('apricot', but it was marrow jam) and said, 'One,' and she said, '*Much* better.'

'Can I get a message home? I've got the priest's number. It's only one and twopence.'

'Oh, I don't think we want to unsettle them.'

'Well, I'll write, then, Mrs Fondle. I promised. She give me the stamp for it.'

'*Gave*,' said Mrs Fondle. She and Harold Fondle then disappeared.

Terry wrote his letter and went to find a postbox, with no success. It was bedtime apparently now and they were sent to a place full of bunks. Two big, plain, confident girls – twins – were to sleep below him. They looked to be eleven at most, but large and commanding.

'You an escort?' one asked. 'You're no evacuee. Not *your* age.'

'I'm not quite fourteen.'

'D'you not want to stay and fight then?'

'I don't know about that. Do you?'

'We're girls,' the other said. 'It would just be in Munitions. I don't want to make bombs for anyone. There must be them like us, over there.'

In the night he heard one of the girls weeping and her sister's head rose up like a vision beside his face on the bunk above. 'Our dad and mam's dead in a raid. Faery's weak. I'm her twin sister.'

*

He rose early next morning, both sisters humps in grey blankets below. He dressed and put on the hooded coat his mother had made him. He was so tall he might have been anybody.

He climbed aboard, up a steep gangway, unnoticed. He walked about on deck. He slipped amidships and soon came to a graceful staircase like Hollywood. Like *One Hundred Men and a Girl*. And high above him on the stair he saw the toes of shiny golden curled slippers jutting over the top step. He found that these feet were attached to the graceful Aladdin trousers of a golden man in a golden coat and purple turban. This smiling man beckoned and bowed.

'Come, little sir. Welcome to the East. Welcome to the *City of Benares*. See what is now before you.'

What was before him was the Arabian Nights. The palms. The languid sun-loungers, the gleaming restaurants, the clean cabins for them all – not only for the paying passengers. The white linen hand-towels, the ballrooms, and everywhere a glorious smell of spices and food he seemed somewhere to have known. An orchestra was tuning up on a white marble dais.

There was a playroom for the little ones, full of toys. A rocking-horse stood there against a wall, its nostrils flaring. It was a strong rocking-horse with basketwork seats fastened one to each side of the saddle, all in wickerwork but very firm and beautiful. Then away went the steward, about the ship. Coloured streamers, big white teeth smiling, princes bowing to Terry as he passed. It must be a film!

Terry felt very much afraid. He was being mocked. He needed to speak, not to his father but to his mother. There were no women on board this ship. They were all princes, all bowing away at him and all false. He had never seen anything like this in the Palace Cinema in Herringfleet.

'I don't think I am meant to be here,' he said. 'Who are you?'

'I am a steward on this glorious ship. It is only one year old. It is known as the Garden of the East. You, all you children, are going to be in heaven. You will be royalty, even the smallest, away from all harm of war. You will eat chicken and salmon and eastern fruit, rich meats, wines, sherbets, bananas and ice-cream . . .'

He was terrified. 'I have to go back. I am not meant to be here. It's a dream.'

'Perhaps the whole world is a dream.'

He ran back on deck. Children were beginning to climb the gangways now in the early morning, some hand in hand, some solemn, some excited, none looking back, none crying. All so little.

On the quay a few flags were being waved. Someone began to sing half-heartedly, 'Wish Me Luck as You Wave Me Goodbye' and from across the harbour, on one of the escort ships which were to come with them to keep them safe, the song was taken up and sailors on her deck began to sing and to wave and cheer. The two stolid twins, big and heavy in what looked like their mother's winter clothes, passed Terry without noticing him. From the inside of the ship came cries of amazed delight, the Pied Piper's children passing inside the mountain.

He asked someone about the Fondles, and was told that they would already have boarded by the private gangway for the paying passengers.

He said, 'I'll go back to the quay then, and find it.'

'No need,' said another golden Indian man in white. 'Come this way.' He had gold tabs on his shoulders.

'I have to go down. I've left my bag.'

'Someone can escort you.'

'I can manage.'

'Hurry then, little master.'

He began to push against the stream of passengers coming up the gangway. He pushed harder, knocking them out of the way, and he was free.

Across the quay, in and then out of last night's dark lodging – his luggage was still there.

'Get *aboard*!' A Liverpool voice. ''Ere – you! You's a passenger – I seed yer. I remember the hair.'

'Just going.'

He pulled up the hood of the coat and half an hour later he was far away, running like mad from the port, wandering in battered, broken Liverpool, looking for a phone-box.

He had the right money and he telephoned Father Griesepert. There was no answer.

He rang Mr Smith's number up in the house on the moor, and – after a long time and the telephonist twice asking if she should disconnect him – little Fred Smith's voice answered.

'It's Terry. Is your dad there?'

'Yer'll 'ave ter 'old on. They'se not awake yet after last night.'

'Get him, Fred.'

'Hello? Terry? Terry!'

'Yes. Sorry, Mr Smith. I'm comin' home.'

'You can't. It is utterly impossible.'

'Well, I'm coming. I have the money from Da.'

'You can't. There's no trains. Middlesbrough Railway Station was destroyed last night. The lines are broken everywhere.'

'Yes. Well. I'm still coming. Somehow. The ship's awash with bairns and little kids and them Fondles is after me. I don't know why, I don't trust them. They think I'm theirs. I'm not theirs. I'm me mam's. And me dad's. I've jumped ship. The ship's about to sail. I'm somewhere in Liverpool. They'll never find me.'

The operator said, 'Your three minutes is up. Do you want to pay for more time?'

He pushed some shillings and then pennies into the slot and after they had clattered down there was silence again.

But then, at last, Mr Smith's voice saying, 'D'you think you can find the Adelphi Hotel? Terry? Very big. Dark. Ask anyone.'

'Yes. I think it's right near. I think I'm beside it. I must have gone in a circle.'

'Go in there. I'll phone them and say you're coming. Right. Now, sit in the main bar there, if they'll let you. Out of sight, if you can. Say someone's coming for you. Say you've had bad news from home that means you are unable to leave the country just now. Give anyone this number. Terry – if this is panic, it may not be too late . . . '

There was a boom like the Last Judgement across the night and the *City of Benares*, its funnels calling out like organ pipes, began its graceful journey towards the Atlantic Ocean.

'It's not panic, Mr Smith. And it *is* too late. I know I'm doing right, Mr Smith. I'm sorry . . . '

'You've been listening to the slaughterer Mr Churchill, forbidding us to run away.'

'No. Look. Will you tell Mam and Da? I'm coming home.'

'You've had your three shillings' worth and more,' said the operator. 'I couldn't help listening. I'm not sure of Churchill neither. Always was a warmonger. Death and glory. I'd go home meself if I was you, lad.'

'Thanks. I know what I'm doing,' said Terry. 'Thanks, Mr Smith. I'm fine.' But his hand shook so much that it took him three attempts to get the heavy black handpiece back on its hook in the phone-box. Behind it he saw his face in the spotted mirror. It looked set and certain. Totally certain.

I look like me da, he thought. So that's OK.

Chapter Fifteen

'Still there?'

The barman at the Adelphi's shadowy and vast main bar was, towards evening, still polishing glasses. Terry was almost out of sight as he had been for hours, around the side of the bar on a black-painted step near the floor, his case beside him, waiting for the telephone to ring.

'You's sure now that he's coming? It's after tea.'

'If Mr Smith said so ...'

'Well, he said there'd be someone coming to get you, not him. Someone nearer, but not that near. From't Lake District. Not nobody, not God, could get over from Teesside today. News travels. It's not in't papers or on't wireless yet. Bombed and flattened the steelworks. First bad un they've had there. We's all but used to it 'ere. You's well away – there'll be more. Aren't you the daft un, not on that luxury liner with the toffs going off to Shangri-La?'

Terry sat on. 'Can I have a drink? A bar drink.'

'I'll give you one small beer.'

'No. I want vodka. I'm partly Russian.'

'I've been noticing the hair.'

'I've been collecting round my school for the Red Cross Penny a Week fund for Russia.'

'Why?'

'I'm a Communist.'

'Oh God,' said the barman. 'Switch off. You've got ground to cover yet. Never mind your father. Hello? Oh, good evening? Yes. Along here. Someone is coming.'

It was a false hope. Terry sat on. He said, 'We never met anyone from the Lake District. Where's the Lake District? I thought it was Canada – like Erie and Michigan and that.'

'By God, you're ignorant. Where you been all your life, Lenin? Herringfleet? Cods-head folk.'

'That's right. Can you get me a sandwich?'

'There's none here to get it for you and nowt to put in it if there was! Mebbe in the police station, if none turns up here for you.'

'Bit longer,' said Terry. 'Mr Smith won't forget. What's that?'

Far away in the main foyer of the hotel there was, drawing nearer, a clear, rhythmic, distinctive mechanical sort of voice. 'Let that be understood. From the beginning. Thank you, yes.' A small man was walking towards them from the far end of the long shadowed passage, talking as if addressing an audience. 'And this is my passenger, I dare say?'

'If you've come from a Mr Smith,' said the barman.

'I have. Good afternoon. Stand up, boy. Shake hands with me. A straight back and a direct look. Good. Good. My name is Sir. Just Sir. I am the headmaster of a school in the Lake District where Mr Smith was once my deputy. All my deputies are called Mr Smith but this Mr Smith is authentically Smith. A fine man. My school is called a preparatory school, or prep school. My Outfit. I'm afraid you are rather too old for my Outfit, but we shall see what can be done.'

('He's a Communist,' said the barman. 'We must discuss the matter,' said Sir.)

'It is a pity that you are so old, for I believe there is much I can do for you. *Hairwise.* (Look up hair in Latin. Roman customs and barbering.) And now what *exactly* is your name? I gather that it is uncertain.'

'Yes. It has always been a sort of uncertainty.'

'It must be settled at once. It is most important. If I can do nothing else I can do that. Venitski? Vanetski? Varenski? Are you all illiterate in Herringfleet?'

'Dad never really discussed it. He came from Odessa.'

('It's Ivan Skavinsky Skavar,' said the barman, and began to sing the tune.)

'Enough!' shouted Sir. 'This is a very serious matter. Your name henceforth shall be Veneering. Yes. Delightful. Polished. In Dickens, Veneering (look up *Our Mutual Friend*) is an unpleasant character, and you will have to redeem him. Veneering has a positive and memorable ring. Rather jolly. You do not look *un*-Dickensian, but you look far from jolly. *So* – let us leave at once. Tonight you will be staying in the Lake District mountains in my Outfit. Mr Smith is coming to remove you tomorrow.'

'Does he know that you will have given me a new name?'

'He won't be surprised. A most sensibly *grounded* man. Has a son of his own, who'll maybe come to my school. Such a pity Mr Smith had to leave me to get married. I have no married teachers in my Outfit. Marriage brings distractions. In my Outfit we are too busy for distractions.'

Handing the barman a crackling flimsy five-pound note, the small loquacious man turned and left the Adelphi Hotel and Terry followed, dragging all his worldly possessions in the suitcase.

'The Adelphi's haunted,' said Sir. 'It is the hotel where

doomed passengers of shipwrecks have always gathered before embarkation. Filled with ghosts and many shadows. Such rubbish. In the back, now. The dickey seat. I don't ever drive with a boy alongside me, for there is always talk in a prep school. Mine is a clean school. Was yours?'

'I don't know what you mean, Sir. Mine was run by a man called Fondle.'

'That,' said Sir, 'is a bad start.'

They roared away towards the Cumbrian fells, Sir occasionally blasting off into the empty night, upon the car's bulbous horn, at resting rabbits. After a time the light around them began to fade into a gentle sunset. Sir stopped the car.

'Bladder relief.

'Now,' he said, 'another day is done. By what I hear it has been a day you are unlikely to forget. Time will tell us if you were directed by some spiritual force of nature, by instinct or by selfish whim. I heartily advise you to beware if it is because of "whim". (Look the word up. Old English, sudden fancy or caprice, *OED*.) Never do such a thing again. Is that understood? I dare say?'

'Yes.'

'Yes, Sir.'

'Yes, Sir.'

'Now, look at the dark hyacinth-blue of the umbrageous mountains. (Check "umbrageous". And "hyacinth" too. They both have a splendid classical root.) Tell me, do you care for birds?'

'Well, I think we only got seagulls at Herringfleet.'

'"Only have." A pity. And most unlikely. Birds can be a great solace. They never love you and you can never own them. Dogs often – and even cats sometimes – can cause pain by their enduring love. Sycophancy (look that up) is never to be encouraged.'

(Who is he? A madman? I like him.)

'And although I wish I could have the privilege of teaching you, you are, as I say, a little old. We stop at twelve or there-abouts. Where are you bound for next, I wonder?'

For the first time it occurred to Terry that he had not the faintest idea.

'I should like to come to your school, Sir, but I don't think there is any money. I stand to inherit twenty-five pounds, but not until my benefactor is dead.'

'Is that per annum, boy?'

'No. It will be net.'

'Ah.'

'I could make an exception,' said Sir, 'but I will not. We might grow fond of each other. I fear that we are unlikely to meet again.'

'Oh! I'm very sorry, Sir.'

'Yes. I have to admit that I am often very sad when a boy leaves my school (though not always). There was one excellent boy called Feathers came to me. Left a year or so ago. Had a cruel stammer. We cured it in a term. He'll be a barrister. You'll see. Rather your sort of calibre. Feathers will have a charmed life and he deserves it, for he had a terrible start. He was unloved from birth. Whereas you – boy – I understand have had a loving home and interesting parents. This will get you through everything. Almost. Because you were loved, you'll know how to love. And you will recognise real love for you. Here we are.'

The school was on a hill up from a lake that gleamed through black fir trees. Boys erupted through its front door and took charge of a large package, the size of a double-bed bolster, which Sir took from somewhere beneath his feet. 'Warm it up at once. Fish and chips. Hake. Irish Sea. Made me late at Liverpool. Hake a wonderful fish, not common. Good for the brain (look up "hake", is it Viking?). God bless our fishing boats. No car here yet? No Mr Smith to take you home? Boys, this is Terry Veneering. Yes.'

The boys were disappearing into the school with the bolster. 'Veneering, you'll have to stay the night,' said Sir, and Terry felt suddenly that it had been a long day.

He stayed for three nights with Sir and there was no message from Herringfleet. He slept in an attic and listened to the birds. He was hauled in to help with football and was a success. In the gymnasium it was even better.

'You may start them on Russian,' said Sir, passing by on the third day. 'We may all be needing it soon. I forbid German, however.'

'I think there's a car, Sir.'

'Where?'

'Standing in the drive. It might be Mr Smith.'

'Excellent. Start now. First Steps in Russian with Class One. Call them "First Steppes" and see if they get it ... I will send for you. You are right. It is Mr Smith. He is approaching slowly. There seems to be a priest with him.'

An hour later Terry was summoned to the parents' waiting room, where a tray of tea and Marie biscuits, off the ration, had been laid out, and Mr Smith and Father Griesepert told him that both his parents had been killed in the air raid on Herringfleet the night he left home. Muriel Street was gone, as were the old rabbit-hole houses in the dunes. Mr Parable was dead along with the people in the ticket office, and nobody had seen Nurse Watkins.

Terry was to leave later that same evening in Mr Smith's car. Father Griesepert was a governor and an old boy of a famous Catholic boarding school in North Yorkshire where, it was hoped, Terry would remain for the next few years.

Terry went, by himself, to see Sir again and found him seated at a desk which looked far too big for him. He was staring ahead.

But he was talking before Terry was through the door. 'Remember,' he said, 'you will not only survive but you will shine. Remember the boy Feathers. You will outshine him. I know. I am never wrong.

'But remember – I am only a walk-on part in your life. This is merely a guest appearance. You will have to get down to your own future now.'

Pompous, Terry thought. Totally self-absorbed. Stand-up comedian. Needs adulation. Probably homosexual. Twerp. No. No.

'And so, goodbye, Veneering.'

'Goodbye, Sir. And thank you.'

'Hurry up. I have work to do. Mr Smith is waiting.'

Veneering turned at the door to shut it behind him and saw Sir staring ahead, his eyes immense, wet beneath his glasses. Unseeing.

Chapter Sixteen

On her Memory Dream mattress sixty years later, Dulcie was listening to the Dorset rain. A sopping spring. At last she heard the swish of Susan's car returning from the station, the front door opening and closing. Some kitchen sounds. The radio ...

(She's taking her time to come up.)

'Susan? Susan? Is that you? Are you back?'

'You know it's me, I'm getting your lunch. Here. Sit up. Soup and cheese. I seem to have been bringing people food all day. Oh, don't *snivel*, Ma. I suppose you've forgotten that I'm going home tomorrow?'

'No, I haven't. Is Herman going too?'

'Where else d'you think he'll live?'

'And I'm not snivelling. It's a cold. I must have caught it in the church.'

'The less said about that the better. Ma – tell me something. Did Fiscal-Smith have some sort of a *thing* about Veneering? I always thought it was Old Filth he was mad about.'

'Thing?'

'Is he gay?'

'Oh my dear! Good heavens, no. He's eighty-plus.'

'He's not related to Veneering, is he? Told me at the station he'd known him since they were eight.'

'Well, they're both from the North somewhere. Nobody knows. The North is big, I suppose. I must say they've both dealt pretty well with the accent. They're both Roman Catholics. Expensive schools and Oxford. Well, for Veneering, anyway.'

'How weird. It's just that Fiscal-Smith, poor little scrap, flipped a bit as the train came in. Made a speech at me about Veneering. *At* me. Eyes glittering. Very odd. He kept pressing that lighted button on the carriage door and all the doors kept opening and closing.'

'Once,' said Dulcie, looking away, 'you were fined twenty-five pounds for that. Pulling the cord for fun. We did it once at school and then we all jumped out and ran across the fields and my foster-family nearly killed me. I wrote to my father in Shanghai to come and rescue me and he wrote back saying he would never write to me again and nor would my mother until I'd written letters of shame to everyone, including the railway company. It was the dear old LMS.'

'Whatever that was. Here, Ma. Eat your rhubarb.'

'I hate the way people call it rhubarb now. It should be rhu-BUB. Only the Queen and I pronounce it properly.'

'When did you discuss rhubarb with the Queen? The last thing – when the doors did close – Fiscal-Smith was saying was that Veneering once had a different name and he was some sort of a hero. Was Fiscal-Smith best man to Veneering, too?'

'Goodness, no! Veneering was married frightfully young. When he was doing his National Service in the Navy after the war. His ship was showing the flag around the Far East. He met and married Elsie ten years before he met the rest of us. Before he met Betty.'

'Yes. We know all about him and Betty.'

'Elsie was Chinese, of course. Never saw anyone so beautiful. But she drank.'

'We know that, too.'

'She was rather after the style of that pink-coat woman at the funeral. Filth's friend. Isobel.'

'Isobel does *not* drink!'

'That will do, Susan! Do you know Isobel?'

'OK – keep your hair on. I used to know her. She liked Herman.'

'*Actually*,' said Dulcie, spooning rhubarb, 'there *was* some link between little Fred Fiscal-Smith and Edward. Something awful. Orphans of some sort. Well, you don't ask, do you? Not done.'

'*I* was a Raj orphan,' said Susan.

'Yes. You made a great fuss. I can't think why. It is such a character-forming thing to be separated from one's parents. I never saw mine for years. I didn't miss them at all. Couldn't remember what they looked like after about a week. But then, I've never been very interesting and I'm sure they weren't.'

'I missed mine,' said Susan.

'Your father, I suppose.'

'No. I missed *you*. Dreadfully.'

'Susan! How lovely! I had no idea! How *kind* of you to tell me. I did write you thousands of letters ... But ... I think I'll get up now and write to Fiscal-Smith. I was a little hard on him for bringing that overnight case. He'll be nearly home by now. I hope there was a dining-car on the train. He remembers – and so do I – when railway cups and saucers—'

'Had rosebuds on them. Yes, yes, we know that. And for God's sake, Ma, don't get up until I've done downstairs. The kitchen's full of damp church vestments.'

And after this, Susan said to herself in the kitchen, thank God, I must start packing for America.

*

Dulcie, not waiting to dress, got out of bed, found some writing paper and sat at her dressing table.

> *My dear Fiscal-Smith,*
> *I am sorry that we did not say a proper goodbye after our little adventure this morning. I had not expected you to leave immediately and I am very sorry if we seemed to be hurrying you away.*
> *Sincerely,*
> *Your oldest friend, Dulcie*
> *PS I don't seem to be able to get, <u>not</u> Old Filth – Eddie – out of my mind, but <u>Veneering</u>. Am I right in thinking that you knew him better than anyone else did? That there are things you never told us? Just a hazy thought. I've so often wondered how he got where he did. So flashy and brash (if I dare say so), so brilliant in court, so good at languages, so passionate and so – whatever they say about him with women – so common. But oh so honourable! Don't forget, I knew Betty very well. But I am saying too much – too much unless it is to a dear last friend, which I know it is. DW.*

And now I am completely restored, Dulcie thought the next day, waving Susan and her grandson off in the hired car for the airport, back to Boston, Mass.

Susan had kissed her goodbye. Even Herman had hugged her, if inexpertly. This visit had been a success! Susan talked of returning soon. Even of sending Herman to boarding school here with the boy his own age over in Veneering's old house, the poet's son. Well, well! I wish she'd say what's happened to her husband. An electric fence around her there.

Today and probably for the next few days, Dulcie decided she would do nothing. It was time for her to be quiet and reflect.

So idiotic at my age, but I must reflect upon the future. 'Reflect' perhaps the wrong word. It has a valedictory connotation. But I am not too old to consider matters of moral behaviour. There is Janice coming to clean on Wednesday and Susan's already done the sheets. I will *not* go over to Veneering's house to see that lovely family. I mustn't get dependent on them. I mustn't become a bore. I shall . . . Well, I shall read. Go through old letters. Plenty to do. Prayers. Wait for Fiscal-Smith's reply.

But when Fiscal-Smith's reply had not arrived by Friday, Dulcie began to think again how much he irritated her. She knew she had hurt him by sending him home, but, after all, she had not invited him. It was that supply of clean shirts she'd seen in the case that she couldn't forget. The image brought others: his ease the night before with her drinks cupboard, his arrogance in the church. How he had criticised the vicar. He knew that the Church of England had to regard their priests as wandering planets now (the current one arrived on a scooter dressed as a hoodie and vanished after the service without a word to anybody), but Fiscal-Smith need not have looked so RC and smug. And so disdainful of St Ague's.

Of course she knew the village was dead. Dorset was dead. It was gone. Submerged beneath the rich weekenders, who never passed the time of day with the local people. Came looking for *The Woodlanders* of Thomas Hardy and then cut down the trees. The only lifetimer in the Donheads was the ancient man in the lanes with the scythe. Willy used to call him the Grim Reaper. Lived somewhere in a ditch – never talked. Some said he was still here.

There was no one to talk to. The village shop, as Fiscal-Smith had not hesitated to point out, was dying on its feet. He didn't have to tell her. She scrapped another letter to him, written this time on an expensive quatre-folded writing paper, thick and creamy, from Smythson of Bond Street – which Fiscal-Smith would never have heard of – and set out on foot to the village shop herself.

It was pure patriotism and she hoped that there were some faces behind the beautiful polished windows and luxury blinds of the weekenders in the lanes to see her. She didn't need anything. Susan had stocked up for her, as if for a siege, in the Shaftesbury Co-op. Dulcie bought at the little shop a tin of baked beans and listened to Chloe discussing whether Scott's oats were better than Quaker when making flapjacks. There rose up a vision of golden heaps of sea-wrack, squid, banana fritters, marigolds and the smell of every kind of spice. A tired, dreamy Chinese chef spinning pasta from a lump of dough for the tourists; a stall piled high with catfish. Mangoes. Loquats.

On the way home she decided to get eggs from the farm. There was a wooden box hung on a field gate. It had been there fifty years. You took out the eggs and left the money. Beautiful brown eggs covered in hen shit to show how fresh they were. Today she opened the flap of the box and there were no eggs and no money but a dirty-looking note saying, *Ever been had?*

She was all at once desolate. The whole world was corrupt. She was friendless and alone. Like Fiscal-Smith she had outstayed her welcome in the place she felt was home. There was absolutely nothing for her to do now but walk back to empty Privilege House.

No she would not! There must be someone. Yes. She would call on the old twins up the lane. The people in the shop had said that there was a new carer there. Well, there nearly always was a new carer there. (Oh! When was the last time there was anybody happy? It's not that I'm really already missing Susan. I wonder if I'd have loved Susan more if she'd been a boy? With a nice wife who would sit and talk to me and play cards?)

She tottered up to the cottage of the old high-powered (Civil Service) twins and was greeted by a dry young woman with a grey face, smoking a cigarette.

'Yes?'

'I am a friend . . .'

'They're having their rest.'

'But its lunchtime.'

'They rest early.'

'I am a very *old* friend. May I please come in?'

Dulcie walked through the nice cottage that seemed to be awash with rubbish awaiting the bin men, and saw Olga and Faery playing a slowish card game at a table. They raised their eyes sadly.

'Thank you.' Dulcie turned to the carer. 'That will be all for now. You may take a break. I'm sure you need one. Please take your cigarette into your car.'

The twins looked frightened. 'She's from a very expensive agency. They said she *did* smoke but not in the house. But she does.'

'It's so strange that we mind,' said Faery. 'We all smoked once.'

'And I suppose we are a horrible job,' said Olga. 'Even though she gets double. She goes on and on about how wonderful her last job was. "Lovely people". She calls them by their first names, Elizabeth and Philip. Do you think it was with the Royal Family?'

'I don't. And if it was, *down with the Royal Family*.'

'Oh, don't start, Dulcie. We're wiser now.'

'I want to kill her. Oh, for some *men*.'

'Don't be a fool, Dulcie, we're all over eighty and we're feminists.'

They sat. The room was cold with no sign of a fire. Faery's legs were wrapped in loose bandages.

'Marriage must be a help in old age,' said Olga, 'but since the husband usually goes first it doesn't rate much now. No penniless spinster daughters at home to look after us either. Must say, I'd like one.'

'Well, my Susan would be hopeless as a daughter-at-home.'

'But she comes and takes charge often,' said Faery. 'You don't know how lucky you are, Dulcie. You never did.'

'But Susan makes me feel such a fool all the time. She's married and clever and well off and has a son and yet she's never happy. Never was.'

'She has her girlfriend,' said Olga, and there was a long pause. The carer was hard at work across the front hall, complaining on her phone at high speed in an unknown tongue.

'Didn't you know? Well of course you must have known.'

Faery said, 'Hugely rich, we hear. And no girl! Woman almost your age.'

'Oh yes. Yes, of course,' said Dulcie.

In the sitting room, the two old women stared at their playing-cards and listened to the carer texting messages (plink, plink) in the kitchen.

'My special subject at Oxford was Tolstoy,' said Faery.

'You don't have to tell *me*,' said Olga.

'Perhaps fiction was a mistake, it has rather fizzled out,' said Faery. 'We should have pioneered Women's Rights.'

'Rubbish,' said Olga. 'It was the wrong moment. Fiction got us through. Fiction and surviving the shipwreck at fifteen years old.'

'Yes. And just look at us now.'

'It's nothing to do with us being born women that we're wearing nappies and in the charge of a drug addict,' said Olga.

'Men get just the same. No family backing, that's the trouble. Poor old Dulcie's an example. Hardly went to school, you know. Married in the cradle. Daft as a brush. Like a school-girl. Silly women haven't a brain to lose.'

'Yes. I wouldn't have wanted to share a cradle with Pastry Willy! He never liked us, you know.'

'No. I suppose we shouldn't have told her about Susan? Nasty of us. Poor Dulcie.'

'Lesbians are always looking for their mothers.'

'It must be hard for them.'

The two old trolls sat over their cards, thinking occasionally of Tolstoy.

Dulcie, having left the aged twins, began to walk home through the lanes, past the infertile egg box, the village shop. When Janice, her cleaning lady, drove by in her new Volvo Dulcie stared at her as at a stranger.

Susan loving someone who is a woman and not her mother! Such an insult to me. I suppose it's been going on for ages and I am the last to know. It was that boarding school at eight, in England, when Willy and I were in Shanghai or somewhere – I forget. I've done everything wrong. I wrote her *hundreds* of letters at school. I did try. She hardly answered them.

But she was so *happy* here in England. All her friends were here, everyone's parents overseas. All seemed so *jolly*. Everyone did it. I can't bear it. I can't bear it. *Lesbian!* I wonder if they all were? I'm sure I didn't know the meaning of the word. Well, anyway, we'd never have talked about it. Men get turned on by divine discontent, and challenged when a woman's mind is always somewhere else, dreaming. I wonder if Betty— No. I heard more than once that there had been something between Old Filth and Isobel, but of course I won't believe *that*. Filth would have had an apocalyptic fit if he'd thought that Betty had ever embraced a woman. Whatever would my mother have thought? Well – I suppose there was Miss Cleaves ...

I'm not sure that the word is apocalyptic?

I wonder who's got Filth's house? And fortune! A woman – Isobel? I saw her in the lanes. Was it yesterday? No – surely not Isobel. There was only ever Betty for Filth. Nobody else. Not ever. Surely? Do you know, Willy (Willy, where are you?), I think I've been left behind.

Oh, is nobody ever virtuous any more – as our mothers were? Well, I *think* mine was. I didn't see her very often – Willy, please tell me. *Whatever* would you make of this?

I suppose, Willy, you never ... ? No. No. Had a—?

You would say, my faithful man (though I was never happy about that lipsticked old Vera), you would say, 'Dost thou think, because thou art virtuous, there shall be no more cakes and ale?' Pastry? Listen to me.

The point is that, as a lonely widow in a big empty house and few friends left (I've forgotten a handkerchief), there is nobody to discuss anything with any more. That is the sharpness of loss. The feelings don't go, even when the brain has begun to wither and stray. I know some very nice widowed people who manage. They manage very well. There's Patsy, laying up dinner places for all her dead relations. Seems perfectly happy. She's got that funny middle-aged son who goes round clearing everything away again. Those with latter-day brains are the lucky ones.

I can't discuss anything with Olga and Faery. Willy would have told me to keep clear of them. They smell of decay. They can never forget that they went to university and they think I am beneath them. They're senile, though. Serves them right for being so patronising. And they only got Upper Seconds, someone said, or was it actually *Lower* Seconds? I bet they both remember that. And I will not leave them comfortless even if they are church-going atheists. I will always be their old friend. I suppose. For what I'm worth. Oh. Oh, dear. I must not crack up.

In the drive of Privilege House stood her rickety car and, finding the key in the lock, Dulcie climbed in and drove away. She reversed, ground the tyres into the cattle-grid, and swept down the hill and up the unmetalled driveway jointly shared by Old Filth's ghost and Veneering's ghost, dividing, one down, one up, and leading nowhere now. She thought: Even those awful rooks don't seem to be there any more.

She accelerated noisily towards Veneering's yews and here, head-on towards her, came a huge crucifix with a pretty woman marching behind it and smiling. Anna.

Anna saw Dulcie's cigarette-lined little monkey face peeping behind the wheel and her expression of panic, and she flung the crucifix aside (it was a home-made signpost), pounced on Dulcie's car and opened its doors.

'I'm just fixing up a bigger B-and-B sign, Dulcie. *Whatever's* the matter?'

'Nothing. The car looked as if it needed a little run. We used to say "a spin". So I'm spinning.'

'You're crying! Come on. I'm getting in with you. Can you drive on up? I'll get you something to eat with us.'

'Oh, but I must get back.'

'Nonsense. Go on. Restart the engine. Don't look down Filth's ridiculous precipice. Stupid place to build that lovely house, down in a hole. I'll bet he had a bad chest.'

She bundled Dulcie into the chaos of her own – once Veneering's – abode, where children's clothes, toys, a thousand books and a thousand attic relics were scattered about the hall and her husband, Henry, was painting the walls bright yellow.

'Hi, Dulcie,' said he. 'Did you know Van Gogh called yellow "God's colour"? Everything here used to be the colour of mud. Bitter chocolate. They were farmers before Veneering. Fifty years. Well, you must have known them? Wanted the colour of the good earth inside as well as out. Hate farmers. Holes in the floor, no heating except a few rusty radiators that gurgled all night, electric fires just one red glow, worn light fittings that blew up. And that's *after* the farmers left. That was Veneering's taste too, and he'd come direct from a skyscraper in Hong Kong. Wasn't an SOP – Spoiled Old Colonial – anyway, whatever he was. What was he, Dulcie? They say he was an ugly old man, bent over. With dyed hair. Dulcie, kiss me!'

'Sir Terence Veneering was my *greatest* friend,' lied Dulcie, stern and angry. 'To the end' (another lie!) 'he was one of the finest-looking men in the Colony' (true). 'Amazing white-gold, floppy hair.' (Henry's was looking like mattress stuffing tied back with string.) 'It wasn't dyed. He could have been a Norwegian or one of those Eastern European people. Odessans? Slavs? He was a glorious man once. But not *dour* – you know. No, no, never. He was noisy and funny and sweet to women, and he could read your thoughts. *Could read your thoughts!* And a constant friend. And – do you know? – we none of us had a notion of how he got to England. Or about his past.'

'Herman says he could play the drums. And the blues. Wonderfully. We're finding revelations in the attics. What do you think – *five* rocking-horses! Come and see. Take anything, Dulcie.'

'And take a glass of sherry with you?' said Anna. 'There's dozens of photographs up there. A lovely boy at Eton and the

Guards. Film-star looks. Very fetching. A somewhat over-the-top boy, I'd say.'

Dulcie said, 'That was the son, Harry. Killed in Northern Ireland. Doing something very mad and brave. It broke ...' (but why tell them? All this past history is mine. And Betty's) '... broke his father's heart.'

'Yes, I thought there was something. This is a broken-hearted house,' said the husband. 'We'll change it. No fears. I wish you would tell us what to do with all his jigsaws.'

'Nobody could really get near Terry Veneering,' said Dulcie. 'Nobody but Betty – Elisabeth – Old Filth's wife.'

'Yes. We have heard about that,' they said. 'Just a little.'

After lunch Dulcie was put back in her car on the drive and, looking up at the house behind her through the mirror, she saw that already it was losing Veneering. There was the same hideousness of shiny scarlet brickwork, the same chrome-yellow gravel and the view at the top of the drive over the miles of meadow was the same shimmering watercolour dream. But the house was coming to life. Below it, Filth's stern phallic chimney still broke the dream apart but from the inside of Veneering's house – doors wide – now came the sound of hearty singing, and the family man (Henry), with his pigtail, exploded across the doorstep in overalls covered with paint and kicking the cat.

'Get out!'

The cat vanished into a thicket.

'Goodbye, Dulcie. Come back soon. Come for B-and-B. We're going to make our fortunes when I've finished painting this place. Cat in the paint tins. Paws no doubt permanently damaged. Colour "Forsythia", like the bush. Horrible colour. Like urine, I always think, but the staircase seems happy with it. We are all going to be, like it tells us in the prayer book, "in perpetual light". I'm never sure about wanting that, are you? Tiring. "Perpetual light".'

'Goodbye,' said Dulcie (They are very self-confident, these people, for newcomers to the village), 'and thank you very much' (but you can discuss things with them and they're not senile). 'By the way, I may not see you for a while. I am thinking of going on a cruise.' (What? Am I?)

Through the driving mirror as she went off towards the road to her own splendid house, she saw them standing side by side, nonplussed. She waved a hand at them out of the car window and laughed. She had her back to them: they could not see the imprisoned girl in her.

Oh, this is not such a bad little place, she thought. Donhead St Ague. It hasn't always been boring like now. It's the cooling of the blood.

The cat rushed out from somewhere and under the car and into the scrub behind the bed-and-breakfast crucifix, and then dashed across the lane. As Dulcie turned towards home she saw it watching her, haughty and yellow-pawed in the bushes.

But it's true, she thought, nobody really knows a thing about another's past. Why should we? Different worlds we all inhabit from the womb.

Chapter Seventeen

Old Filth, Terry Veneering, Fred Fiscal-Smith.

Two accounted for, life completed.

And in the shadows, like a little enigmatic scarecrow, Fiscal-Smith, the one born to be a background figure.

Fred Smith lived, all his boyhood, in the same lonely Yorkshire landscape. Each day, he saw to his mother, who was an invalid and almost always in bed. Fred got himself to and from school from a bus stop down in Yarm. His father (its headmaster) left the house at 6 a.m., often to walk with his bike to the school along the shore. A splendid headmaster but a cold father.

And Fred? After his success at secondary school and evening classes, and the deaths of both parents ... silence.

Twenty years on.

Now, Fred Fiscal-Smith is a qualified lawyer living alone.

Scene I: Lone Hall, near Yarm, North Yorkshire.
Hour: Just before sunset.

Month: October.
Year: Say, 1955.
Set: A room, upper floor of large, tumbledown, scarcely furnished house where, at a window overlooking the sea, a young man FRED sits upright at a desk, back to audience, writing a letter. The wide window he faces shows racing sky.

Below are the great chemical works of the North-East, a thousand narrow chimneys, each one crowned with an individual tulip flame. They stretch from the estuary to include the remains of the old back-to-back houses and the older fishing village of Herringfleet.

Pan to a dreary town, jerry-built over bomb damage of twenty years before. Trees that once marched along the ridge of the Cleveland Hills are limp and dying and stand out black and tattered as reminders of an ancient domain. Only the sea survives unchanged. It frames the shore of the flat and sorrowful landscape. It swings out. Swings in. For the letter-writer it is silent, and distant.

FRED FISCAL-SMITH is writing a letter with a fountain pen (ink Swan, Blue-Black). As he writes, light is slowly fading from the sky which by the end of the scene has left darkness outside and the windows a splash of black light. Lights have begun to show across the estuary. A tiny flat, waltzing blue flame tops each of the forest of chimneys.

The smell of the chemicals rolls across the land and more disgustingly as night falls. Letter-writer holds handkerchief to his face. (Handkerchief white cotton. Large and clean. Marks & Spencer, new high-street store.)

Letter:

To Terence Veneering, MA (Oxon)   *Lone Hall*
Herringfleet
Yarm
North Yorkshire

My dear Terry,

This is a letter of congratulation on the news I see in today's <u>Times</u>: that you have passed out top in the Bar Finals examinations and are henceforth to be revered as the best-qualified lawyer in England and life member of Inner Temple.

But perhaps you don't remember me? We haven't met since our early schooldays. Nor have I heard of you since 1941 – 15th September, as I recall, two days after the air raid when my father and Father Griesepert came to collect you from somewhere in the Lake District and took you to your new school, Ampleforth College: a few days after you had so cleverly, providentially, jumped ship, the <u>City of Benares</u>, as she set sail to drown, or rather cause a German U-boat to torpedo and drown, over a hundred people, most of them children, in mid-Atlantic and including your headmaster and his wife, the Fondles.

I did not come with my father and Father Griesepert to find you, but stayed with Mother, who was ill. We were inland from the bombing of the coast and here I still reside. I breed a few Highlanders.

I have never set foot in Ampleforth College although it is nearby. I went to Middlesbrough Grammar School and then to Middlesbrough Tech a few miles from home. I too have become a barrister, but on the despised Northern Circuit. It serves me well.

My parents are dead. I still live (alone) in the old house that looks across to Herringfleet and the sea, and its only disadvantage is that it is far from the railway. I am less prosperous than you people in the South but I am still in touch with those at the Bar, and I go to stay with them as often as possible. I very much hope that you and I might meet again? Trains from York are frequent and I can get to York with the aid of a series of buses.

It has taken me a little time to realise that Terence Veneering MA (Oxon) is the Terry Venetski (or Varenski? How insular we were!) of my schooldays. You made a wise move, to my mind. There are some very dubiously named members of the Bar at present, many of them dusky.

You would not recognise Herringfleet. Nothing is left of what we knew. No slum terraces, no cooking on the fire-backs. Muriel Street? Ada Street? Who were they, Muriel and Ada? No weekly animal sacrifice for the Sunday joint takes place in the slippery back alleys. You may well remember, just before the War, some of us coming with bowls to buy the blood? A salt-black – a black-salt – <u>smell</u>?

There followed after the War the smell of the chemical works. It was very toxic, but we sat it out. It rolled down the coast and up here into the hills. I wish some artist might paint the chemical chimneys. There will be no record left soon. The poisons here are now muted, though still released at night. As tonight.

Some sort of phantom of the smell rolls yet along the coast and up here into the hills at nightfall when they

hope we are asleep. And all the trees along the
Cleveland Ridge – Captain Cook's statue you will
remember? – are dying.

If you do think of returning for a visit however, there
is an excellent hotel in Yarm. It was once the judges'
lodging, where they all stayed on circuit – maybe for
assizes, I don't know. Sometimes, even now, you can
come upon nostalgic members of the judiciary
drowsing there on vacation and hoping for some
decent conversation. Rather terrible vermilion and
ermine portraits grace the staircase. It is a place where,
if you visited, I should be delighted to come if you
thought of inviting me to dinner?

But first, of course, it would be pleasant to come and
stay with you in London in your hour of glory.

Sincerely yours,
Fred Smith

PS You will see from the Law Lists that I am now
known as Fiscal-Smith. Fiscal is my own invention, as
(perhaps) Veneering is yours?

Scene II: Fade to a dark place under the rafters of a brothel
and above a dodgy dentist's on Piccadilly Circus, London.

The room is unfurnished except for books and a canvas bed
with a metal frame. Coloured lights swing past its dirty window all night long: a released rainbow after years of wartime
blackout. Noise of traffic and shouting continuous. The noise
of post-war, but still threadbare, London trying hard for joy.

Figure (TERRY VENEERING) is lying on bed fully clothed.
It has long blond hair. It is very drunk. The room is carpetless.
The washbasin is blocked.

A bashing on the door. The figure on the bed, top of the lists
of the International Bar examinations of Great Britain and the

Commonwealth, puts a cardboard box over his head and shouts that he is not in.

GIRL's voice: It's not the rent. I've got a letter for you.
TERRY VENEERING: Money in it?
GIRL: How should I know? Come on, I'll cook you a dinner.

Silence falls. At last footsteps retreat. Outside, the crowds are screaming in Piccadilly Circus, the ugliest piazza in Europe, for the return of the statue of Eros, the god of love, removed for safety during the Blitz. The lights revolve upwards and in the rafters it is like a lighthouse. Round and round.

Slowly light fades away and noise of crowds, too. From this tall and narrow old house behind the hoardings you hear only the odd occasional street-fight, tarts shouting, students singing. Lights, lights, lights, after the years of darkness, still seem a daring extravagance. The blond man on the canvas bed groans.

The letter from Fiscal-Smith has been pushed under the door. Terry Veneering has no shilling for the meter and it is cold. He staggers about. Finds a cigarette. Takes letter to window in case they've cut off the electrics. Reads letter.

It is from a man even lonelier than he is. This shows in the reader's face, which softens slightly. (Voice-over of letter, here perhaps?)

Then he moves, finds paper to reply. There is only a defunct and grubby brief, long settled out of court.

Dear old Fred,

Well I never! Thanks old chum for the congrats. Often wondered what became of you. I went up to Oxford for five minutes before the War. After school – RC Ampleforth College, fees paid in full by the school itself. Thanks to old Greasepaint (remember?). Then Oxford again after the War. National Service, showing the flag around the Med. In white and gold and proud salutes. Nothing nearer heaven than then! The girls at all the ports, all waving us in! Malta – oh Malta! The priests shook holy water over us. And the processions and the flowers! Mind you, the mothers made the girls get home by nine o'clock for Mass next morning. Every morning! Hard to leave behind, Fred. Hard to leave. I'll go back one day. Place to die in. (I'm a bit drunk.)

I waved goodbye to the ship off the Point, near Valetta, and waited for passage home, when, bugger me, RN sends me off again to parade ourselves around the Far East to show that 'England is England Yet' (pah!). Married there. Yes. Chinese girl – very rich. Boy born rather soon. Harry. I am not of the Orient and, I guess, a weird son-in-law.

My wife Elsie (yes!) is said to be the most beautiful woman in Hong Kong. She has a bracelet round her wrist of transparent jade. There since birth and will be all her life. It was the transparency of the seamless jade did it for me. God, I am drunk, Fred Smith!

By the way – look again. I was not top of the Bar Finals. I share the silly honour with one Edward Feathers. I expect you've heard of him? Or know of him? We were at Oxford together on return visit – cramming – after the War. We hardly spoke. He was the Olde Worlde star of the Oxford Union and I was never called upon to open my mouth there in debate because I am <u>louche</u>, Fred, <u>louche</u>. Feathers is one of those born to the Establishment. Cut in bronze, unfading. <u>Big</u> connections I've no doubt. He dominated his year. No time for the Arts. Neither

drinks nor wenches. Bloody clever. We hate each
other – God knows why. We pass each other now in
the Inns of Court without a word. He of course has got
Chambers already. I am still cap in hand – wig in
hand – but I can't afford a wig. Nor a cap, come to
that.

I can think of nobody I would have preferred NOT
to share an honour with than Eddie Feathers.
Remember Harold Fondle? No – he's not as bad as
that; but he has the fatal APLOMB.

Feathers is Prometheus. He is thoroughly,
wonderfully good. The idea of sharing an honour with
him is almost as terrible as that of sharing a woman
with him. I cannot however think that this could ever,
possibly, happen.

Also – how I run on! – he was at the prep school
where I would have given almost anything to go to.
Where your father taught once, Fred. Man in charge
called 'Sir'. Met him when your dad came and rescued
me when I had run away from being an evacuee (and a
corpse) on the City of Benares. *Feathers was Sir's star*
student. Sir clearly in love with him. Well, well, 'this
little orb'. In-it amazing?

Why am I so full of hate for this man Feathers? 'He
hath a certain beauty in his life/That makes mine ugly.'
We'll go to a Shakespeare together, shall we, Fred?
When you do come down to London? If I can afford a
ticket. There's Olivier being something or other in St
Martin's Lane. Sorry. I'm drunk. Did I say that
before?

Oh yes – don't expect to stay with me. I'm sleeping
on the floor at present. There's no respectable
accommodation to be had in London unless you have

Oxford 'connections'. No doubt Les Plumes of this ghastly world have. By the way, how interesting that you are 'breeding Highlanders'. Do they wear the kilt? Do you know Bobby Grampian?

London's a bombsite, Fred-boy. Stay among your stinking chimneys.

Love from
Terry

Curtain to some solemn music.

Chapter Eighteen

Terry sat in the Law Library of the Inns of Court, looking at the envelope addressed to Fred Smith he had found in his pocket. It had been there for nine days. Letter to the dreaded Fred of yesteryear, the meanest boy in the elementary school by the sea. He wondered about putting a penny or a penny-halfpenny stamp on it. Penny would do. He had few enough. F. Fiscal-Smith, Lone Hall, near Yarm, North Yorkshire. A really merry-sounding address.

Think of swotty little Fred turning up! Well, well. And a lawyer. Post it when I go out. On the way to the interview. Why ever did I write so much to him? Terrible bore when he was eight. Will be worse now. Lawyer. Of *course* a lawyer! Well, he can't come and land down here with me. I'm on the pavement.

Tonight would be the first time Terry Veneering had no bed to go to. The landlady, so-called, in Piccadilly Circus had said as he left the house that morning, 'Oh, yes. There'll be another man here tonight. I told him I thought you wouldn't mind sharing.'

'Well, you were wrong,' he'd said, slamming upstairs, picking up his case, crashing out of the front door after leaving four shillings on the hall-stand.

Where to go? Think about it in the Law Library. He'd already been the rounds of the few people he knew in London. Might try Bobby Grampian. Lived in Kensington somewhere, with his mother. Thoroughly nice man. No side to him.

'Hello? Oh, *hello*! So glad you're in, Robert. It's Terence. Yes, Veneering. Yes. Oh, thanks. Well of course I'm only joint top with Feathers. No – I haven't actually met up with him lately. Listen, Bobby, you once said if I was ever stuck for a bed in London – could I possibly stay tonight? I've an inter-view for a place in Chambers around five o'clock in Lincoln's Inn and nowhere to sleep. I'd be gone by breakfast.'

Silence. Then, '*Tomorrow* night is that, Terence? *Tomorrow* night?'

'Well, actually tonight. My landlady told me this morning that she thought I wouldn't mind sharing – with a stranger. So I ...'

'Good God. That's terrible. Of course you're welcome. Delighted. I'll just check with Mother. We're having a bit of a party here tonight. Scottish dancing. We've a piper coming. I don't suppose you have the kilt in your luggage? No? Well, never mind. Can lend.'

'Actually, I haven't much luggage at all. Toothbrush sort of thing.'

'We have some splendid people coming. Do you reel?'

'Well, no.'

'Never mind. I seem to remember that you play?'

'No! Well, saxophone. Bit of the blues. Piano.'

'Oh, well. Shame. Just come. Not too early. Or late. Mother has very early dinner and goes to bed at nine.'

'Actually, could I come another time? I can't be sure of times tonight – I mean this evening – you see. Depends on how long this interview's going to last. I'm looking for a seat in Chambers – anywhere, of course, will do.'

'Where's the interview?'

'Oh, just general. Libel and Slander. Nothing distinguished. Not sure where. It's on a bit of paper. Tutor at Christ Church set it up.'

'Be careful. Libel's a vile life. Come some other time, won't you, Terence?'

'Thanks.'

'Oh – and do you sing? Madrigals! Next week ... ?'

'Not very well, Bobby.'

'Oh, pity. I live at home here, you know. Shan't bother with Chambers, not just yet. Bit nostalgic for the old days after three years in the German nick. Picking up the old life ... '

Veneering crossed the Strand, the letter to little Fred in his pocket. He dropped it into a letterbox on the corner of Chancery Lane and thought of it being opened in the despoiled – and by him never revisited – Cleveland Hills. It was late afternoon now and the fog had come down. He thought of Malta gleaming at dawn. Thought of Elsie's jade bracelet, her creamy skin, the star-tlingly beautiful little boy, Harry. Veneering was wearing his only suit, his demob suit, which was already getting shiny. Hideous. Cold. He was hungry. *No room at the Inn*. Ha-ha.

Why in the name of God did he want a job as a working courtroom lawyer? In a set of Chambers nobody had ever heard about? Because he was up against war heroes and wealthy young men. Because there were ten applicants and more for every vacancy. He remembered Elsie's terrifying family. Suffocating, alien. And rich. He knew why he had to try everything that was offered in London.

He found the Chambers and walked in.

*

The clerk – a very famous clerk, he had been told: Augustus, the kingmaker – looked him up and down and said, 'Oh yes. I remember. All right, I'll see if he can see you. He's very busy,' and vanished, pretending to yawn.

Then, 'Follow me.'

'Mr Veneering, sir, of Christ Church College, Oxford, and new member of the Inner Temple, starred First, top of Bar Finals, introduced by old tutor, an old friend of these Chambers.'

The tall, dapper Head of Chambers, very scarlet about the face, shiny-lipped, found his way from among the crowd of young men, all drinking wine and shouting with laughter. 'Mr *Who*? Oh, yes, yes, yes. Mr Veneering. Your tutor – he was mine, too, you know, I'm younger than I seem. How unbelievably young you all look now despite the recent conflict. I hear that you have travelled about the globe? Showing the flag? What a joy. All our troubles ended by the dropping of the splendid atomic bomb. Your – our – tutor never thought much of me, you know, yet here I am at last proving myself useful to him. Soaking up the latent talent of our great college. He says you're Russian? I don't think – I'd better say at once – that these are *quite* the Chambers for a Russian. Have you tried one of the more *unnoticeable* professions? Perhaps the Civil Service?'

Veneering said that he was a lawyer.

'Well exactly. *Exactly*. But we are exclusively Libel Chambers here. We are, I'll admit, on the verge of being fashionable – even royalty hovers – but all is very slow and fragile. So *very* few decadent duchesses. *Huge* sums to be made of course eventually, but, dear boy, not yet. Tell me, why did you become a lawyer?

'Someone said I'd make a good one. He left me all his money. He wasn't born rich. He qualified down here in

London living on ten shillings a week. He set up offices in various parts of the country for worthy chaps like me. He was a sort of saint.'

'Oh, I'm afraid he would never have been in the swim.'

'No, he wasn't. As a matter of fact I'm living on about ten shillings a week myself.'

'He was a member of the *Bar*, this benefactor?'

'No. Just a solicitor. In the North-East. He was killed in an air raid. His name was Parable—'

'I can't believe it! It is *pure* John Bunyan! He can't, if you don't mind my saying so, have left you very *much* money if you have to live on ten shillings a week?'

'It turns out that my inheritance has gone missing. His house and office both took direct hits in the North in 1941. I received only twenty-five pounds in notes from someone unknown, and a letter saying all his other assets were to be mine when I'd taken Bar Finals. I have my Royal Navy pension of two hundred a year.'

'Oh, my dear chap – yes, thank you, Hamish, just up to the top – and he impressed you?'

'Of course. He made sure I left home and didn't get killed in the same air raid he did. I was en route to Canada as an evacuee—'

'Oh, my God! What dramatic lives we have all led. Thank your stars you weren't torpedoed aboard the *City of Somewhere*. All the little babies floating upside-down in the water like dead fish. Depth-charged. Wonderful accounts of the few survivors plucked from the debris. Upturned boats, basket chairs – even a rocking-horse! *Not* very sporting. Now – just a minute, Toby ...' and the red-lipped man walked Terry out of the room, a manicured hand around his shoulder. 'Dear boy, I would *dearly* like to have you. Have you tried other Chambers? You have? Ah well, you know, the chance will come. Give it time. There's no work anywhere at present. Nobody sane is going to Law. The price of victory is lethargy and poverty. We must bide our time and use our private money. I'm sure you'll find Mr Parable's treasure somewhere. But as you can see ... As you can hear ...'

The noise and the odours of bibulous men, the cigarette smoke, the good white Burgundy followed Veneering out and back into the stately planting of Lincoln's Inn Fields.

'I have simply no room for another pupil,' said the Head of Chambers, shaking hands. 'Dear fellow, how I've packed them in already! I've got them swinging from the chandeliers!'

'So!' said Veneering. 'Ha!' and he walked across the grass and up to the stagnant static water tanks set in place years ago to deal with the coming fire-bombs on the Inn. Nasty things, floating. 'It has come to this. A stagnant country, threadbare, idle, frivolous, cynical. Hidden money.'

He longed for Herringfleet. For his shadowy father, his amazing mother, for Peter Parable. For high-mindedness. For the coal cart. He kicked his feet in the tired grass.

So much for the Law. The Law is still a ass, as the great man said over a hundred years ago. Dickens. Lived near here. Must have had a splendid view of the Law in action, when you think about it. Five or ten minutes' walk from his house now in Doughty Street. I'll go and see it. I'll go now. I'll pay homage. I'll prostrate myself on his study floor and I'll say, 'Dickens, you did what you could. (And why didn't you get a knighthood? Queen Victoria liked you. Was it the infidelity?) And you did a lot. And you changed it without a Law degree. You did it on your own with a pen and a bottle of ink.'

I am not going near the Law now. I'm going to be a journalist. A left-wing journalist. The *New Statesman* offices are up at the end here, up the alley. I'll walk in now. I'll demand a job.

And I'll be given one. I feel it in the wind.

Back in the Libel Chambers the clerk, Augustus, was pushing his way through the throng of the party. Finding his Head of Chambers he said, 'Sir? Where is he?'

'*Who?* Augustus, have a drink.'

'Him. The foreign fellow. Looking for pupillage?'

'Oh, *him*. Goldilocks. No good, Augustus. Useless. Too odd. Too foreign.'

'You never sent 'im away, sir?'

'Oh, he wasn't desperate.'

'But *we* are desperate, you fool, sir. That one's a winner.'

'Now then, Gussie, how d'you know?'

'I'm a clerk. I know what I can sell. He's young and fit and he misses nothing. Brilliant. Better qualified than anyone in this room. You've lost us all a fortune, you bloody fool, sir.'

'Oh, don't say that! Get him back then, Gus. We'll take him on. I'll write to his tutor.'

'He won't come back. Not that one. It's "love me or leave me" with that one. You'll hear of him again all right, but he'll always be on the other side. That one's a lifetime type. Not that he'll want much truck with Libel and Slander now. It'll be the Commercial Bar for him, he's poor. You've lost him his beliefs, about helpless widows and orphans. That one's for Lord Chancellor. He'll be on the Woolsack if he wants to be. I feel like going with him. You dolt, sir.'

'Oh dear! Augustus – Augustus, have a pint with me later in the Wig and Pen Club.'

Veneering walked away from the static water tanks on Lincoln's Inn Fields and towards the offices of the *New*

Statesman and Nation where he would, of course, be taken on immediately. Then he would take a short walk to Dickens' house in Doughty Street, a handshake with his ghost, then cadge a lift somehow back to Oxford to recover his books, lecture notes and dissertation, then burn the lot . . .

After which . . . Back East, and into the iron grip of Elsie's family business.

Oh!

Towards the north end of Lincoln's Inn the crowds, en route to their buses and trains home to north London, were tramping beside and behind him. Crowds tramping south towards the river and Waterloo Bridge and Station were advancing towards him in similar numbers. Nobody spoke or smiled or paused. Old Square.

But Terry Veneering stopped dead.

He stopped dead.

The crowds washed around him, one or two people looking up at his pale face and glaring eyes and platinum hair. (About to faint? Hungry? War casualty? Mad?) One grumbled, 'What the . . . ?' and stumbled and another said, 'Bloody hell! You had me nearly over.'

Terry turned and began to walk slowly back with the southbound throng, retracing the last twenty or so yards. Then he stopped again, turned again and looked across, fearfully, at the building to his right. There was a little patch of old garden, its railings taken away years before to make Spitfires, a scuffed stone archway with a scuffed stone staircase twisting upwards. Up the first two steps of the staircase, on the wall of the old building was a faded wooden panel with its traditional list of the names of the lawyers who had worked within. The list was far from new, but painted in immemorial legal copperplate. He read the words PARABLE, APSE & APSE, SOLICITORS.

*

The door was not locked. He walked straight in, expecting a derelict store-room, fire-buckets, stirrup pumps, tin hats abandoned since the Blitz. Just inside he saw instead a row of iron coat hooks where someone had hung a bowler hat and folded a pair of clean kid gloves on top of it.

Terry opened an inner door without knocking and facing him sat a young man at a desk, a sandwich suspended en route to his mouth. Beside him on a smaller and more splintery desk stood a gigantic Remington typewriter on which were arranged a pocket mirror, a paper napkin, paper plate and similar sandwich. A middle-aged woman wearing a fake-fur coat sat behind it.

Jaws ceased to move. Eyes stared.

Terry said, 'I believe that you are a firm of solicitors?'

'Ah,' said the young man, putting the sandwich down on a clean handkerchief on his desk. 'Not exactly! Not for a few years. We are in a state of flux. But may we help you?'

'You must know – have known – Mr Parable? Mr Peter Parable?'

'No, sir. I'm afraid all the old partners in the firm are dead. We keep the names on the door in the old tradition. It is rather like the memorial friezes on the walls of the tombs of the Pharaohs. I am a very, *very* distant Apse. Thomas.'

'And so this is – a set of Chambers?'

'Well, no. For years it seems to have been a solicitor's office. One of a string of almost charitable centres for the poor – an early Legal Aid – set up by the founding Parable, a Northerner. A lonely philanthropist who made a considerable amount of money.'

'And he . . . ?'

'Was killed in the war. We are in the process of being dispossessed by the Inn. Desperate for space. Work here is rather slow and no one is really in charge. All Mr Parable's fortune was left to someone quite outside the family with a strange name, and he is dead.'

Very carefully, Terry sat down on an upright chair with one leg missing and propped up by books.

He said, 'I should like to negotiate for the tenancy of these Chambers.'

'I'm afraid it is quite impossible,' said the woman in the fake fur. She delicately tore her sandwich apart with her pink fingernails.

'My name is Veneering.'

'Oh yes?'

'I was born Venetski.'

'That has a *ring*,' she said.

'I am the one who inherited Mr Parable's estate. Though he never promised me more than twenty-five pounds.'

After he had finished his sandwich the young man repeated, 'I am Tom Apse, a very distant relation just keeping the premises open. And this is my secretary, Mrs Flagg.'

She nodded and picked up her knitting. She said, 'I'm afraid that buying these premises will be impossible, Mr Venetski. We will of course inform the Inn of your offer, as we do for everyone else who comes in. Our only safeguard up to now has been that Mr Apse is an *Apse*, like on the door. To keep them off ...'

'And,' said Tom Apse, 'upkeep for *any* tenant will be astronomical. And I have my Egyptology to consider, and Mrs Flagg – well, she has Mr Flagg. I'm sorry, sir, in spite of your interesting name – I'm sure we've heard it before somewhere – you won't be able to make a case for yourself. Old Mr Parable's heir was drowned at sea in 1941 on the evacuee liner the *City of Benares*.'

Terry stood up.

'I am that evacuee,' he said. 'Except that I wasn't. I had a premonition and good friends.' (The world is singing! The light of heaven fills the sky! Dear God! Dear Sir. Dear Father Griesepert.) 'I changed my name.'

Tom Apse and Mrs Flagg also rose to their feet and the three shook hands.

'At present I am without money,' said Terry.

'Then how do you think you can buy this?'

'Borrow,' said Terry. 'There must be security somewhere. And a proper search. There doesn't seem, if I may say so, to be much paperwork about the office.'

'We get few clients,' said Tom Apse. 'We pass them on. The Apse archive is very daunting.'

'You must consider us *caretakers*,' said Mrs Flagg, 'as the desultory fight drags on. The cupboards and the cellar are full of paper, though some of it is still dampish after the Blitz.'

She arranged her coat around her shoulders and on high heels rocked towards the wall, where she opened a cupboard and watched several shelves of documents, tied up with tape that had once been red, vomit all over the floor.

'Work to be done! We'll start tomorrow,' said Veneering. 'Now, the three of us are going to the Wig and Pen Club. Right NOW!'

'Sir,' said Tom Apse, 'I'm sorry, but – identification? We only have your word. How do we know who you are?'

'You don't,' said Veneering. 'Put your coat on fully, Mrs – I can't call you "Mrs Flagg". What's your—? Daisy. Oh, pretty. Come on, Tom.'

'But *money*, sir?'

'Mr Parable lived on ten shillings a week. I haven't broken into next week's yet and I'll be sleeping here free tonight if we can find a hammock.'

*

In the Wig and Pen Club in the Strand sat the red-lipped Libel Silk with friends. He rose at once and came across.

'So delighted to see you again, Mr – er ... I have been sending out search parties. I find that I have a place for you in my Chambers after all. My clerk, the Great Augustus, is very cross with me for not making myself clear.'

'Too late!' Terry shouted, signalling a barman. 'I'm fixed up. I have inherited a sleeping set of Chambers of my own.'

'You are fixed up? Already? You'll find it a very lengthy business, on your own. Takes years. Ask anyone about the Parable, Apse fiasco, for instance. A disgrace. Dragging on. Quite Dickensian.'

'Well, I have an inheritance looming. Fallen, by the grace of God, into my lucky lap. Meet my secretary, Mrs Flagg – and my junior clerk, Mr Tom Apse. I have a good senior clerk already in mind.'

'I'm afraid, Mr – er – you have simply no idea! It will take a lifetime.'

'Yes. But I'm young. I have wide connections, you know, especially in the Far East. And thanks for the interview. And thank Augustus. Tell him I shan't forget him.

'I don't forget anything,' he added. 'And now Mrs Flagg and I are off to buy a bed.'

Dizzily on the pavement Daisy Flagg burst into joyous tears. 'Oh, come *on*,' said Terry, spinning her around. 'Beautiful coat. Is it real?'

'It's only coypu,' she wailed happily. 'It's only a superior kind of rat.'

'When I come into my kingdom,' said Terence Veneering of Parable Chambers, Inns of Court, 'you shall have sables.'

Chapter Nineteen

And so Terry Veneering was established in his own Chambers as if by angelic intervention. And so began the long, slow, interminable legal process of disinterring his Parable inheritance.

He was never one to reflect on the meaning of life. Or the shape of his own life. He knew that from childhood he presented the figure of one certain to succeed, charm, delight and conquer. Not for him the grave, moral pace of the gentlemanly Edward Feathers.

But had he ever considered doing anything as deadly dull as writing an autobiography, he would certainly not have chosen today as its pivotal point. He would have chosen the day, some six months later, when he had had to scrape the bottom of the judicial barrel down at the Brighton County Court alongside the beginner, little Fred Fiscal-Smith, and against – needless to say – Edward Feathers: the case of the over-sexed lion tamer's apprentice. For that was the day Veneering realised that he had no stomach for Crime.

*

Stepping out of Victoria Station at the end of that dreadful day, his heart sank even further, for in London there was fog. London fogs were getting worse again. During the war, coal had been rationed. Now coal was back, and fogs swirled about the East and West End. They nuzzled and licked and enwrapped you in yellowish limp fleece. They stained your clothes, your hair, got up your nose and down your ears. Your chest wheezed. When you sneezed, your handkerchief was dark ochre. You muffled your mouth. You coughed and coughed.

It was only when they stepped out of the *Brighton Belle* on Platform One that the three lawyers realised that, during their day in breezy, wholesome Brighton, the fog in London that had hung about for days had reached Dickensian proportions. It had turned into 'The Great Fog'. It might last for days. It was also getting dark and there was no transport of any kind to get them home.

Old Filth was all right, he lived just round the corner in his spartan, curtainless apartment where there were two small electric radiators, and Fiscal-Smith suggested that he might stay the night there as well.

Veneering – in case the ever-polite Feathers asked him to stay too – announced that he would go to the Goring Hotel, near Buckingham Palace and not more than two minutes from the station.

He set off holding his arms out in front of him, his briefcase between them, thinking vaguely that somewhere there would be a taxi. He immediately vanished. Any hotel was way above his means, let alone the Goring. So as a matter of fact was a taxi. The brief fee for the lion tamer's boy had been seven guineas – the shillings to go to Tom Apse as clerk – and anyway it hadn't yet been paid.

London had fallen into the silence of death and all its lights were gone. Abandoned cars stood in the middle of the road. Occasionally a shadow trudged past him, emerging from and disappearing into the mist like the ghost of Hamlet's father. London had lost its voice.

Taking twenty minutes to cross into what he hoped was Grosvenor Street, he collided with an elephantine shape standing lightless and empty. It seemed to be a bus. He turned from it, thinking that this was going to be slow, and stepped in front of a car whose lights were smudges. He thought the nearest Underground station would be the only hope, and cannoned into a lone newspaper boy shouting a cracked refrain – '*Star, News, Standard*' – to nobody.

'Goin' far, guv?'

'Inns of Court.'

'You'll not be there by morning.'

'How are you getting home then?'

'I'll doss down the back of the statue.'

'What, Marshal Foch?'

'Don't mind which marshal. Any marshal. Marshall and Snelgrove. Cheers, guv.'

It was three hours later that Veneering reached Fetter Lane. There were a few flares burning here and there and along the Strand in front of the empty shops and restaurants. He went almost hand over hand towards Lincoln's Inn – what he hoped was Lincoln's Inn – decided that it couldn't be, clutched at some masonry beside him and toppled upon the steps of Parable, Apse and Veneering.

He fell inside. He found a light. He slammed his front door upon the murk. There came a flash of memory of a blue sea – his sunburst of life in the post-war Navy. His – hum, yes, well – his wife and lanky little boy.

In the office the fire was not lit but a sack of coals stood beside the shabby old grate. There was nobody now to tumble the coals down to the cellar via the coal hole in the road and nobody to drag it up to the grate from the cellar. He kept his in the sack, covering it with a blanket on the few occasions when anyone called. But too late – too tired – to light a fire tonight. He found a bottle of whisky in the cupboard and some cream crackers, and swigged down the whisky.

Coal, he thought.

He thought of the threat that the government were to ban coal fires in London and he thought of his mother. He informed her and asked for her opinion, but received no answer. The fog had entered the house with him. It was wreathed above his head. It smeared the window. How it stank.

'Mam – I'm packing this in. The Law. I've an interview with a paper. Foreign correspondent.'

'Your collar's filthy,' she said.

'It's the fog.'

'Steep it and wash it. You've got an iron?'

'You lived by coal.'

'I'd no option. You have.'

'I need sleep.'

'There's time to sleep and there's time to waken.'

Veneering crawled across the floor towards the stair that led to the office he used as his bedroom. 'I'm drunk, Mam. I want to go to bed.'

'You'll do it. Remember your father.'

'He had you.'

'Well, you have me, too.'

The knocking upon the front door had the desperate, dogged quality of a long assault. On it went, on and on.

At last, 'Message,' said a youth Veneering had not seen before.

'What?' Veneering peered blearily round the door.

'Message for Mr Veneering. Urgent. Reply essential. Shall I step in?'

'No,' said Veneering, taking the note and shutting the door on the boy, feeling about in the dark vestibule, finding the door to the office, groaning and grunting. He read:

Mr Veneering. Appointment this morning, 30th April, ten o'clock at no. 21, St Yves Court, Gray's Inn. Respectable dress essential. Clear head. Mr William Willy will see you for interview for possible place in new Chambers at present being established. Anticipating overseas connections. Reply to boy. Signed: Augustus.

'Nobody could be called Mr William Willy,' said Terry Veneering. 'On the other hand ... the Great Augustus – I'll put my head on the block to it – has never made a joke.'

Oh, well then. Shame. After yesterday's fiasco in the world of the eternal circus, he's too bloody late, Augustus. I go a hundred miles to defend a poor little gormless insect who tickles ladies' private parts as they're sitting enjoying the lions and tigers, and he gets three months! *Three months* for a bit of harmless fun. Clearly I'm not cut out for Crime. First and only time most of them ever got tickled. Great Grandee Edward Feathers has palpitations of shock-horror. He's never tickled anybody's legs. Never will. *Gross* indecency, etc. Is this what we got our First Class honours for? 'Pom, pom, pom' honks Feathers, county court moron judge nodding in support, all his chins wagging like blancmange. Fuck the English Bar, I'm off to the *New Statesman*. Journalism for Veneering. Get the words about the world, not into the fly-spotted Law Reports. Sorry, Augustus, Willy is too late. I'm dressed for a different play. I am about to approach the political rostrum.

He opened the outer door. 'You – laddikins – take a note back saying I'm busy.'

'I can't do that, sir.'

'And for why?'

'Because Augustus has you in mind. You can't *not* reply to Augustus, Mr Veneering.'

'It is, I know, very early in the morning but could you just try to realise, BOY, that even you are not the slave of this Olympian monster? Whoever he is – you are not in his THRALL. There are many barristers in thrall to their clerks. There are *judges* in thrall to their clerks ... I am my own man, boy, I make my own choices. Thank Augustus and say I have a previous engagement.'

He shut the door and listened to the boy marking time on the stones on the other side of it. After a while the boy rang the bell.

'YES?' Veneering immediately flung it open. 'YES?'

'You better come, sir. Nothing to lose. Much to gain. And Augustus – well, you don't want 'im for your enemy, now do you?'

'Oh, well then. OK,' said Veneering, 'OK. Say I'll come. Soon. Better shave. I've a very important interview this morning already, at the *New Statesman and Nation*. Tell Augustus. And tell him that to be summoned before someone called Mr Willy sounds an unusual command.'

'Yes, sir. Shall I wait and take you round?'

'Whatever,' said Veneering, slamming the door, stamping up his stone spiral stair, surveying himself in his fur-lined waistcoat, pink open-neck shirt, tight black trousers, brown boots, long platinum new-look hair. He stared at the mirror for some minutes.

The boy had disappeared when Veneering eventually emerged into Lincoln's Inn and its water tanks. Ah well. Got the message. *New Statesman* first priority. The Literary Editor there a woman. Sounded daunting. Not young. Apparently somebody. Chat her up. Who's afraid? Not I who knew Mrs Veronica Fondle – and I drowned her! This one had said on the phone that she promised nothing except a sandwich together in Lincoln's Inn Fields sitting on the grass to talk about his future. 'You sound so very young, Mr Veneering. Did you not think of staying at Oxford – life as an academic?' (She ain't seen me yet!)

No, Mrs Beetle-Bags, I did not. I don't want to interpret the world, I want to put it straight. To spread the globe out flat like pastry on a slab like Ma made. Pick it up, slap it down, turn it over like a tarte Tatin in Le Trou Normand in Hong Kong. Oh hell, that was wonderful! I don't want a careful bloody life. Why am I turning to the right? This place in St Yves Court – St Yves, the Breton lawyer. And saint. (Might write a book on him?) Augustus's chambers . . .

. . . Where there is nothing but a gaping door and windows and a heap of rubble on the pavement with a rope round it and a red lamp you light with a match. And it's eight years on. 1953 – Christ! However did we win the war? No one will ever know. I'll tell my grandchildren.

Or will I? Will I reminisce? Will they give a fuck for historic Britain? Little ragged-edged, offshore island and not my country anyway. Go to Russia soon, let's hope. Everywhere fighting their neighbours to the death. Death doesn't bring life – ever.

He saw his housemaster at his Roman Catholic school saying, 'Sharpen up, Veneering.' The Resurrection? Oh, fuck.

He took his eyes off the heap of rubble and looked up steps to a tall row of early-Victorian houses where doors and window frames gaped empty. In front of each house was a heap of rubble similar to that at his feet: beams and floorboards and shelving and corner cupboards and lead fire-backs. Nearby there was a marble chimneypiece. It had a small deep-carved circle at the top of each pillar. Around 1740, he thought. He lusted after it. A man was loading all the rubble into a lorry.

'Can I have that?'

'What – that broke fireplace?'

'Yes, how much?'

'Take it for free. How you goin' to get it home?'

'I'll manage. Leave it aside.'

He stood looking at the silken marble skin under the grime. Smooth as jade. He saw the translucence and perfection of the surface under the dirt of the war. He thought there must always have been people who stared at such things. He imagined his wife's terrifying family at her birth, fastening the tiny jade rings around her baby wrists. Her shackles. He thought of his mother, pushing tripe about in the black frying pan on the coal fire. Her worn hands. He thought of all that his mother had had no knowledge of. Her tiny world where she, among all her family and friends, had pondered and sought helplessly for explanations, alone.

Augustus was standing on the top steps of one of the unrestored houses. At the bottom of the steps near him, a bike was propped on one pedal, its basket on the handlebars full of flowers. A girl pushed past Augustus and came running down the steps towards the bike. She passed Veneering like a whiplash, but he had the impression of happiness, good temper, laughter, excitement. She leapt on the bike, balanced, kicked the pedal and hurtled away out of sight. She was barelegged, sandalled, in a crazy new-look skirt that did not suit her (legs a bit short – though good). She had not seen him.

Augustus called from above, 'Please come in, Mr Veneering. I *hope* you are in time.' A dreadful look was cast upon the fur-lined sleeveless jacket.

'Mr Willy can see you now. I hope.'

But there seemed to be nobody there.

The room was large but far from ready. The windows were newly glazed but still with builders' fingermarks. There was no carpet. Bookshelves were not yet filled. There was a big plain desk with little on it except an enormous concoction of cellophane wrapping with a bunch of spring flowers in the midst, and a book.

A voice said, 'My god-daughter left them. The girl you were watching getting upon her bicycle.'

The man was small with a pasty face and sitting rather out of the light in an alcove beside a roundabout bookcase. He had a sweet smile.

'I'm so sorry. I didn't see you.' Veneering found that he was tugging down the waistcoat. Pushing back his hair.

'Veneering?'

'Yes, er ... you sent for me.'

Mr William Willy said, 'I have been asked to establish a new set of Chambers for specialising in Engineering and Construction Law. There is soon to be a great deal of building work – "skyscrapers", bridges, roads – which we hope will continue to be in the hands of British lawyers. English engineers are still very much the best, except for the Italians, and in Hong Kong and Singapore, for instance, there are some huge contracts brewing for what we call "the Far East" and the Americans call "the Orient", which shows a certain romanticism in them, I suppose. I am Shanghai-born, Mr Veneering. I am not a romantic. I understand you speak Mandarin? And you are a travelling man?'

'Well, only post-war Navy. Round the China Sea. Showing the flag. Yes, I do speak Mandarin. I find languages easy.'

'Are you prepared to travel?'

'Yes. I don't have many allegiances.'

'But you have a wife and small son in Hong Kong, Mr Veneering.'

After a thoughtful space Veneering said, 'This isn't generally known. But yes.'

'Would you stoop to practise in the construction industry? They often call it "Sewers and Drains". High fees, international experience, but you would be doomed to personal obscurity. No honours. No Lords of Appeal.'

'I haven't really thought ... '

'About whether or not you care about obscurity?'

The pale-faced man walked to the window behind his desk and turned his back on Veneering and looked across London.

'You haven't really started thinking yet. You and Feathers.'

'If you are inviting Feathers,' said Veneering, 'then I'm not interested.'

'And nor, I'd guess, is he. He has connections of his own. You of course could become an academic. Or you would make a very good journalist. Maybe at the *New Statesman*? I expect you are left-wing? But you – I have made enquiries – like money. Do you also like power?'

'This is like the night I arrived at Ampleforth and the monks grilled me,' said Veneering.

'Ah, yes. That was when the *City of Benares* went down. You were very lucky to escape. Have you second sight, Mr Veneering? That is always useful. You might be very useful all round.'

'I don't talk about it. No – I jumped ship because ... I wanted to go home. But I thought nobody had been told about that business.'

Augustus came in and took the god-daughter's flowers away to put them in water, leaving the book.

'Your name is not really Veneering, is it?'

'How ever do you know that ... ?'

'Because I know my Dickens. You can't use a good name twice. It is a joke. Veneering was a *nasty* man ... '

'I haven't actually read—'

'But you are *not* a nasty man. I knew your father. His name was Venetski. Was it not?'

Silence.

'Your father, whatever his name, was, I think, from Odessa? A blond Odessan. An exceptional person. He had been a hero. Then he was left totally alone for years, at great risk, abandoned, crippled, fearless to the end. They got him, of course. Not that I am suggesting for a moment that the whole purpose of the German air raids in the North-East was to eliminate one defunct – shall we say specialist – er, thinker? Political activist? Your father was a great man.'

Veneering said, 'Are you telling me that my father was a spy?'

'I'm telling you, Veneering – Venetski – to come and work for me in . . . in the construction industry.'

'And have this.' Pastry Willy handed the book that the goddaughter had brought across the desk. 'I have any number of copies. *Life's Little Ironies*. Thomas Hardy was a builder and architect by trade, you know. In the construction industry.'

Out on the street – a very thin brief in his jacket pocket – Veneering flagged down a taxi and persuaded the driver to heave in the fireplace. Then he opened the book and read on the fly-leaf, *To my darling godfather Uncle Willy, from Elisabeth Macintosh.*

Chapter Twenty

During their last year on earth in the Donheads, Feathers and Veneering drew slowly together, step by hesitant step, as they walked the lanes around their village. First they had pointedly ignored each other from a distance. Later they had nodded and looked away. Then came the famous Christmas meeting when Feathers had shut himself out of his house as, cut off from the rest of the world by a snowfall and the Dorset earth beneath his feet beginning to freeze, feeling Death clutch at his wheezy throat, seep into his ancient bones, at last, hand over hand, up Veneering's drive he went, from one branch of Veneering's dreary overhanging yew trees to the next, until he had dragged himself, ancient, decrepit orphan of many storms, to Veneering's peeling front door.

Nobody locally – nor anywhere else – ever discovered what went on during the rest of that Christmas Day, but afterwards the two old men met regularly in Feathers' (much warmer) sitting room in his house down their joint driveway, for chess. Chess and a drink. Or two. But never more (though we don't know what Veneering did back home up the slope, later in his lonely night).

Feathers never offered food. Nor did Terry Veneering ever suggest a return visit up the slope.

Their chess improved, their concentration deepened. The photograph of old Feathers' dead wife Elisabeth (Betty), with whom Veneering had been in love since he first set eyes on her on a bike outside Pastry Willy's office – and beyond her death, for he was still in love with her – surveyed the two old men from the mantelpiece.

It was a flattering photograph, taken on a picnic on Malta where she and Feathers were completing their honeymoon half a century ago.

That day for the young couple (he had bought her a fat crimson and gold chair in a back street in Dacca during the honeymoon) had been a day of blue and gold on the clifftops; the sea, far, far below – St Paul's Bay where he slew the serpent – running bright green.

There has always been on Malta the belief that there is a crack in the clifftop where a fresh-water stream runs silver. It trickles down the slope, falls, sprays out into the dark. Far below, a spout of spittle shining like light above the ocean. Betty the bride had said, 'There! You see! There *is* a fresh-water spring dropping down to the shore.'

And the girl had stretched herself out and looked down through the crack, her legs out behind her. Her legs were not her best feature. They were Penelope's legs, not Calypso's – but they were brown and sleek and strong and her pretty Calypso feet had kicked up and down and she lay, watching the clear water turn to mist. She had shifted slightly and the water shifted slightly like a net. It revealed a very small glimpse of the creeping emerald tide below.

*

Sixty years on, comfortable in his winter sitting room, fire blazing, whisky coming along any minute and – ha-ha! – he'd taken Veneering's queen – a sweet peace fell upon Edward Feathers, and for the first time since he'd acknowledged his wife's infidelity with this jumped-up good-looking cad he knew that his jealousy was over and that he could now look back over his life – and at his beloved wife – with pleasure and pride.

Well, perhaps not. Perhaps love shall always be divorced from time.

What a delicious, young and merry face looked at him from the mantelpiece. The trophy of his successful life.

And only a photograph.

She was not necessary to him any more.

Betty had never been a siren. There had been one or two of those, and he smiled kindly at his young self – oh, almost possessed by that other one. Isobel. She must be gone by now. *She never told her love.* They say she only loved women. Rubbish. Did I rewrite my will? I expect she's gone by now. All shadows.

But potent shadows. We strengthened ourselves, Betty and I. Isobel weakened me.

But sometimes I do mix them up.

On the whole, he said, addressing an audience of some great court, I managed well. Better than Veneering and his idiot adolescent marriage. How lonely that shrill Elsie must have been. She left him, of course, and the boy didn't love her. If we are honest, it was Madame Butterfly who left Pinkerton (I say, that's rather an original thought) and Veneering knew his weakness. He knew from the beginning he was not the man he might have been.

'Veneering,' he said, 'checkmate, I think? Yes? Whisky now – you ready?'

Silence. Then Veneering saying, 'Yes. Good idea,' and continuing to stare at the board.

'Tell me,' said Filth, 'that's to say if you have no objection – how did you get yourself entangled with Elsie?'

There was such a long silence that Filth looked down into his glass, then up at the ceiling, then winked at Betty's photograph and wondered if he had gone too far.

Or maybe Veneering – God, he was ugly now, too – was becoming deaf. He had rather wondered. Didn't appear to be listening. Filth looked keenly now at Veneering's ears to see if there were any of those disgusting pink lumps stuck in them like half-masticated chewing-gum. Thank God no need of that himself.

No sign. What's the matter with the man? Sulking? Thinks I'm prying. Not answering.

'Sorry, Veneering. Shouldn't have asked. Never even asked you about that shipwreck incident you were in. *City of Benares*? They tell me you were in a lifeboat for twelve days and only a child. Amazingly brave.'

Still silence. A coal dropped in the grate. Then Veneering moved a pawn with a smart crack as he put it down. 'Checkmate to me, I think?' He picked up his glass and drained it at a gulp.

'Elsie?' he said. 'Do you really want to know about Elsie, Filth? More dignified if you'd never asked. Rather surprised at you. And I wasn't a hero of the *Benares*. I ran away before she sailed. Not brave at all.'

'Good God, it's not what we all believe.'

'Ran off across Liverpool till I heard her hooter sounding off goodbye. Three days later she was torpedoed. Well, I probably wouldn't have drowned. Some didn't. Two in this village didn't. Those fat twins. Never speak. They were the heroes. I was sent away afterwards to a Catholic boarding school – I'm Catholic – because my family had copped it the same night in an air raid. Then I started at Oxford and got called up for National Service post-war.'

'I missed that,' said Filth. 'Done the Army. Older than you.'

'Then off to the Med in the RNVR. Six months' paradise. Every port. Showing the flag. God, the girls! Standing scream-ing for us on every quay. No reason not to spring into their arms. No Penelopes sitting sewing blankets back home and wishing we were there to take the dog out. Heavenly. Then, just about to sail for Portsmouth – floods of tears and gifts and promises of eternal love – and they sent us *on*! *On*, out East to the Empire of the Sun. Hong Kong. Singapore. Unbelievable pleasure. Sun. No chores. Splendid naval rations, enough money, Tiger beer and all of us like gods, bronzed and fit and victorious, dressed in white and gold. Parties at governors' resi-dences. Parties, parties. I never read a book. I never thought beyond the day. I had no home to hurry back to. I met Elsie.'

'I remember her.'

'Oh, yes. Singapore. She was – well, you saw her.'

'Not until about ten years later. She was so beautiful. To me she was beyond desire,' said Filth.

'D'you remember,' said Veneering, 'how, when anyone saw her for the first time, the room fell silent?'

'Yes.'

'Chinese. Ageless. Paris thrown in. Perfect French. Poise.'

'We all wanted poise in women after the war. The women who'd been in the war were all so ugly and battered. The rest were schoolgirls and they slopped over us. We thought nothing of them. We were looking for our mothers, I think, sometimes. Beautiful mothers. Was Elsie like your mother?'

'No. My mother was a figure from – from beyond the Ural Mountains.'

'She gave you your blond hair?'

'No. Not exactly. She could have organised the Ural Mountains.'

'Elsie . . . ?'

'Just stood there at some meaningless party. Tiny pea-green silk cheongsam. Made in Paris. They were rich. Her father hovered. Seldom spoke. Watched me. Had heard I had a future. Knew I had a bit of a past but could speak languages. Bit of a reputation at Oxford . . . Knew I had no money. I needed, *wanted* money. Women – well, enthusiastic. He invited me with the family group – I didn't know that – to a dinner to eat crabs in black sauce. Everyone shouting and clacking Chinese. I was already good at it. Showed off. Unfortunately got drunk – but so did they. So did Elsie. She wore these little jade bracelets on her wrists, fastened on to rich girl-babies. Tight, sexy. Just sat there. You know what it's like. Round table. Non-stop talk. Suddenly all over and everyone stands up. Shouting. Laughing. Family – well, you know, unbelievably rich and – well – cunning. I found myself taking her home. It was considered an honour.'

'You needed an old friend, Veneering, to get you out of that one.'

'Yes. D'you know, I remember thinking that it would be good if Fred – little Fiscal-Smith – had been there.'

'Well, I had to go back and marry her.'

'Couldn't old Pastry Willy and his Dulcie have helped?'

'Not then. Well, they might have done. But Willy hadn't yet taken me under his wing. I doubt if he'd have wanted to know me. I was swimming through life after the war. (Yes, thanks. A small one.) You were pushed into it in those days by – well, by the Church. There is a Catholic church in Singapore. It survived. It was thronged. It was home. Somehow you keep with it. And so amazing that Elsie was Catholic. Or so she said. And a few months later we had a son.'

'I remember your son. Who didn't? Harry.'

'Yes. He was a wild one. He had my language thing. I sent him to the same English prep school as the Prince of Wales. Elsie's family flew him back and forth. He was— He was such a *confrère*. Such a brilliant boy . . .'

'I remember.'

'Then they thought he was dying. Cancer in the femur.'

'I heard something . . .'

'Betty – your Elisabeth – well, you must know. Looked after him. Back in England. Tiny, wonderful little hospital in Putney. I couldn't get there in time.'

'And his mother?'

'Elsie was in Paris. A hair appointment.'

'And after that, you still stayed with Elsie?'

'It turned out it wasn't cancer. Yes. Well. I stayed with my boy.'

'I'll walk you home,' said Filth.

'Elsie died,' said Veneering, 'an alcoholic.'

'I am so sorry. We did hear . . . But you had the boy.'

'Oh, yes. I had the boy.'

'I had no child,' said Filth. 'Come on. Bedtime.'

'Your supper smells good,' said Veneering. 'My mother could cook.'

'I never knew mine,' said Filth. 'Now, are you all set for your visit to Malta? Strange place. I envy you,' and he waited to see if Veneering would say, 'You should come with me.' But Veneering did not.

'Actually,' said Veneering, 'Elsie got very fat.'

'She needed your love,' said Filth.

*

But late that night, after his orderly, reflective bathtime, the evening lullaby of the rooks harsh and uncaring, Filth thought: He needed more than Elsie could give. He needed Betty. And Betty was mine.

The next morning Veneering's hired car for the airport swished along his drive at six o'clock and he didn't even look down at Old Filth's great chimney as they sped by. It was raining hard and still not really light.

And this black and wintry morning in this cold rain Filth was realising that, at last, he was seeing Betty from a little distance. As a man, not even loving her particularly. Seeing her away from this English village, thick with history, hung with memories like those ghastly churches in Italy hung with rags. Rags and bandages and abandoned crutches, abandoned because prayer had been answered, wounds all healed, new life achieved. Betty Feathers lay dead in Donhead St Ague churchyard. The monumental husband was, at what must be the end of his life, turning out to have a persona apart from his wife. Level-headed, a comrade, all passion spent. Urbane enough to play chess with his lifelong sexual rival – and forget.

What idiot years they had passed in thrall – whatever thrall is – to this not exceptional woman. Not a beauty. Not brilliant. Stocky. What is 'falling in love' *about*? And her attitude to life – it was antique.

She could love of course, thought Veneering. My God, I'll never forget the night she was with me. And she said so little.

When I think of Elsie! All we hear about the silent, inscrutable Chinese! Elsie screamed and screeched and spat. She flung herself up and down the stairs in front of the servants. Hecuba! All for Hecuba! Didn't care who heard her. Put little

Fiscal-Smith off women for life. Went white, as he watched her. Bottles flying. Jewels flung out of windows. How flaccid she became. Rolls of fat. She had the bracelets cut away. Her wrists began to bulge and crease. She couldn't understand English – not the words. Her 'English' was faultless. But what it *meant*! In Chinese for her there was no innuendo, irony, sarcasm. Bitch-talk she could do. She asked Betty, who was in her twenties, if she was a grandmother and Betty said, 'Oh yes, I have seventeen grandchildren and I'm only twenty-seven,' and Elsie had no idea why she said this. The most hateful thing about Elsie was her fragile hands. She would pose with them, cupping them round a flower, and sigh, 'Ah! *Beautiful*,' and wait for a camera to click. Life was a performance. A slow pavane.

For Betty it was a tremendous march. A brave and glorious and – well, comical sometimes, endurance. All governed by love. Passion – well, she'd forgone passion when she married. Her own choice. She'd taken her ration with *me*. She wouldn't forget that night. Hello – Heathrow? Still raining. Why the hell am I going to Malta for Christmas?

Throughout the network of the cobbled streets of Valetta the rain poured down, turning them to swirling rivers. There was thunder in the winter rain. No one to be seen. Cold. Foreign. Post-Empire. Oh, Hong Kong!

Veneering was staying in what had been the governor's residence. The hotel, a medieval palace, stood blackly in a courtyard that was being bombarded by the rain and the huge doors were shut. Veneering had sat in the taxi and waited while the driver with a waterproof sheet on his head had pounded at them and then hung upon a bell-rope. At last, after the flurry of getting him in, Veneering tipping the genial driver well – but not receiving quite the same excessive gratitude as long ago – he stood in a pool of rain on the stones of a reception hall that rose high above him and disappeared into galleries of stony darkness. He was then led for miles down corridors with here and there only a vast stone coffin-like chest for furnishing. The odd frail tapestry.

The dining room reminded him of the English House of Commons, and he was the only guest. The menu was not adventurous. There was a very thick soup, followed by Malta's speciality, the pasta pie, the pie-crust substantial, and then a custard tart. A harsh draught of Maltese red wine. There was no lift to take him back to his room which was huge and high, the long windows shuttered, the bed a room in itself with high brocaded curtains that did not draw around it. In one of them a hole had been cut for the on-off switch of a reading-lamp that stood on a bedside table that was a bridge too far. The sheets were clean but very cold. Rain like artillery crashed about the island. He lay for a long time, thinking.

But in the morning someone was grinding open the shutters and the new day shone with glory. Palm trees, brown and dry but beautiful, rattled against a blue sky and racing clouds. At breakfast, with English marmalade and bacon – and bread of iron – there was a pot of decent tea strong enough for an old English builder. A man on the other side of the breakfast room, with another pot of it, lay spread out like a tablecloth over a rambling, curly settee. His feet reached far into the room. He said, 'Hello, Veneering. It *is* Veneering, isn't it? I'm Bobby Grampian.'

'Good Lord! Yes, I am Veneering. I'm said to be unrecognisable.'

'Not at all. We're all said to be unrecognisable. It's just that there's no one much left to recognise us. Staying long? I'm here with Darlington.'

'I used to live near there.'

'No, no. Chap. Darlington. Just his name. Viscount or something. Always been here. He wants to be a barrister's clerk. He'll be delighted—'

'Hasn't he left it a bit late? I've been retired about twenty years.'

'Eccentric chap. Lives in the past.'

'Are you still dancing? I mean reeling . . .'

'Oh God, yes. Never without the pipes. Mother's gone, I'm afraid.'

'Well, yes. Are you in the same house?'

'Where you came that night? Kensington. Splendid evening – or was it the Trossachs?'

'Actually I never quite got there.'

'Remember you doing the reels— But you inherited those marvellous Chambers! People pay to visit them now. Listed. Apparently once belonged to John Donne.'

'John Donne? The poet?'

'Wasn't he the King of Austria?'

'No, I don't think so.'

'Yes, "John Donne of Austria is marching to the war". Dear old G. K. Chesterton. He was a Catholic.'

'I think that was Don John.'

'Yes? I'm very badly educated. Very sexy man, John Donne. Sexy poetry.'

'He was Dean of St Paul's.'

'Extraordinary. To think you inherited a royal dwelling. Sold it, I suppose? Get rich quick. What d'you think of this hostelry? Bit like after the war. What a funny new-old world we've lived through.'

'Well,' said Veneering, 'it's large and cold. I came here for Christmas cheer. A break from Dorset winter.'

'Alone? Oh, most unwise. We must get together. There's a

Caledonian Club, I'm sure, and I have the pipes. Ah – and here's the man. Here's the man!'

Unchanged since Betty and Edward Feathers' honeymoon, a shambling person shuffled towards them demanding porridge. 'Hello?' he said. 'Know you, don't I? Golf? Are you on your own?'

'It's Veneering,' said the Scot.

'Oh.'

'Veneering. The retired judge. Friend, no, contemporary, of the great Filth. Come here for a Christmas break.'

'Ye gods! Very few of us left. Splendid. Anything special you want to see? Some wonderful ancient tombs, and so on. And the skeletons of pygmy elephants. No?'

'Well, I would rather like to see the cliffs again. There was a fresh-water spring.'

'Place we used to go to for picnics. Very *British* place. Take you there now if you want. You'll be able to see to the horizon and down to the depths. Heaven and hell, ha-ha. You coming with us, Grampian?'

'No thanks.'

'Ready then, Veneering? Porridge good here, isn't it? Actually, Veneering, I have something to ask you.'

'Yes?'

I've always had a hankering to be a barrister's clerk. Don't know why. I can organise, and I like the ambience.'

(He must be eighty!)

'You may have heard of me. Always around.'

'What was – is – your profession?'

'Never had one. It wasn't a thing all the expats wanted after the war, you know. Bit knocked about. Prison camps and so on.'

'You were in one of the camps?'

'Not actually. A good many friends. Pretty upsetting ... I

ought to write my memoirs. Trouble is, I haven't many of them. Getting on a bit! "Riff-raff of Europe", they used to call the English in Malta after the war, but actually I think we are harmless. Just rather … *poor*. Not unhappy.'

'And you must know everybody?' said Veneering.

'I know the villagers of my village. And a good many ghosts. Could be worse.'

The exile from Darlington stopped his ancient Rover on a hairpin bend at the top of a steep slope. He laughed heartily and began to lead Veneering across a rough terrain of scrub.

'A bit slippery,' said Veneering. He looked about him. There was nothing but underbrush. Up above there was a circle of unfinished housing, ugly and raw, little stone gardens, scarcely a tree. Standing by itself, at the very edge of the cliffs, was a small rose-pink palace with stonework of white lace.

'Eighteenth-century,' said the would-be barrister's clerk. 'For sale. Dirt cheap. I could arrange something if you were tempted. Here we are. Stretch yourself out on your belly and you might see the silver stream. Runs underground most of the way. Then it falls towards the sea. Noise like choirboys singing. Mind you, I haven't lain out flat on my belly for a long time. No one to appreciate it – ha-ha. Not sure I'd know what to do now with a woman even if she was all laid out like lamb and salad, as we used to say. We're all impotent here, you know. Don't know what's become of us all. If you ask me what we need is another good war.'

Veneering moved further off. The stones beneath his unsuitable shoes became sharper. Twice he stumbled into what might be a fissure in the cliff but saw and heard no running water. He decided to crawl about and dropped slowly and painfully to his knees. He put his ear to the rock.

'You're a game old bird,' said his companion. 'You know,

the last time I was here was over half a century ago. Picnics up here were special. Planned months ahead. Time of "the six-penny settlers". More money than ever before. Each other's houses, or sailing. Lots to drink. Fornicating. We came up here once, though, for a sort of honeymoon party. That arrogant old bugger Eddie Feathers (Old Filth they call him now, and I wouldn't disagree) had his bride Betty with him. Should have seen his face when I asked him to arrange a clerkship for me.

'As for her! Never forgot her. I was sitting cross-legged with my wineglass and she was standing right beside me, and she dropped on her knees and looked down the crack. She was like a kid. And she splayed herself out and I patted her bottom and she was up like a kangaroo, and she *hit* me! Yes, hit me. Don't think he saw. On their honeymoon it was. She said, "I'm going to get out of this. I'm going down the cliff to the sea," and she went off and him after her. Old Filth. Mind you, *she* was the one who I'd have thought not exactly pure as a lily. Nasty stories about her going off with some man. Even though she looked like a schoolgirl. *Oh*, yes. She stepped on me! Small of my back. Expect Filth knew she wasn't all she might have been. Hey, what's the matter? Stop that. What have I done?'

Veneering's pale fist had clenched and cracked into the monster's jaw. Both men fell sideways and began to shout and yell.

Away over at the rose-pink palace some Germans were being shown round by an estate agent. They called out. One of the Germans looked through his enormous binoculars and said, 'It seems to be two old men fighting. It looks like a fight to the death.'

Across the seaside tundra there came a snapping sound and the thin old man with streaks in what had once been golden hair was lying still, one leg apparently missing. It had invaded the terrifying opening in the cliff from which the fresh water poured into the ocean.

'Locally it is called the water of life,' said the estate agent, but when they reached the two combatants this did not seem apt. Veneering's ankle was broken, his foot hung limp and he had passed out. He came round only briefly when mobile phones had summoned help and he was being carried off on a stretcher towards the hospital. Before he died, after a thrombosis had set in, he told the would-be barrister's clerk that he wasn't having one word said, ever, against Elisabeth Feathers.

When Old Filth heard the news he said, 'Silly old fool. Off on a jaunt like that at his age. I'd not have gone with him even if he'd asked me.'

Then Filth sat out the long day and the evening in Donhead St Ague, listening to the rain, not looking up behind him to Veneering's darkened house, not bothering with whisky or the television news or the supper left out for him in the kitchen. He sat on and on in the midwinter dark.

When a postcard from Veneering arrived – written his first evening in the tomb-like hotel – Filth read how happy he was there, with no desire to come home.

'So he did get to heaven, then,' said Old Filth to his wife's photograph on the mantelpiece, and Betty's young face smiled back at him from another world.

Chapter Twenty-one

In Donhead St Ague half a century after the honeymoon picnic, the family man and poet, hard at work clearing Veneering's attic, his wife Anna cooking and laundering for her burgeoning bed-and-breakfast business, their children at school, their cat with activity of its own. A raw cold day and nothing in the village stirring. The family man appears in the doorway of the ironing place holding a battered photograph.

It is of a lipsticky young woman with bouffant hair. The photograph has been stuck long ago on cardboard and its margins covered with kisses.

'Veneering again,' he says. 'I wonder which this one was? I'd guess it isn't Betty Feathers.'

Anna takes it and turns it over. She reads, '*From Daisy Flagg with love and gratitude.*'

'Isn't she lovely?' says Henry, the family man (and poet). 'Like a juicy fruit.'

'But she's not his floozy,' says Anna. 'My head on the block, she's not. I wonder what he did for her. That's a fine fur coat.

I'd guess a secretary of some sort. Adoration in the eyes. I'll take it round to Dulcie. She'll know.'

But they forget, and the photograph is put aside on a window-sill and then upon a pile of books and then tossed in the rubbish collection. A week later Anna yells at Henry to take the rubbish to the gate before he leaves for a poetry festival next day and he sees the photograph again and stands in contemplation. He says, 'Anna – all this stuff in the attic and there's not a sign of Betty Feathers anywhere. Not a letter. Not a postcard.'

'Men are like that,' she says. 'I don't expect her husband kept anything of hers either. It's women who press flowers in books. Keep letters.'

'Do you? Will you?'

'No. Because I've got you.'

'Don't be so sure. I might run off with Dulcie.'

Then he left the photograph on the kitchen table and went off to the tip. When he came back he said, 'We haven't actually seen Dulcie lately. Go and show her this while I'm away.'

'Isn't she on a cruise?'

'Oh, we'd have heard. Janice would have told us.'

'Janice is on holiday. Two – no, three – weeks. D'you know, I don't think we've seen Dulcie since that day the cat went mad. I'd better go round. She'll be on her own. The dismal daughter is back in America with the eccentric yoof.'

'Go tomorrow after I've left. The sole of my shoe's hanging off. You're better at sticking it back on. And I've not finished my lecture.'

'Sorry,' said Anna. 'There's glue somewhere in a box. I'm going to Dulcie *now*.'

*

And she knocked and rang, although both the kitchen door and the front door of Privilege House stood open. She walked in, stood in the quiet hall and called, 'Dulcie.'

Deep silence. Her neck prickled. The house felt cold, unoccupied. In the kitchen, a slowly dripping tap. Everywhere empty of life.

In Dulcie's bedroom her bed was unmade and the floor strewn with old clothes, probably sorted for a charity. Looking again, Anna saw the crumpled expensive wool suit and the black funeral hat. There were some tiny antique corsets. White cotton stockings like Victorian fashion plates. However old *is* she? Are these menstrual rags? Virginia Woolf used menstrual rags. She only died in 1941. Dulcie must have been planning a fire, like the cremations on the *ghats* of the Ganges.

And she is gone.

Then through the open door at the end of the landing she saw Dulcie's childlike back, very upright at a writing-desk that faced the fields and empty sky. She appeared to be writing letters. Thick yellow paper around her feet was crumpled into balls.

'Dulcie! Good heavens!'

She waited for the little figure to keel over sideways from the current of air disturbed by her voice; to slide to the floor. Dead for weeks.

'Yes?'

'Dulcie! You're freezing up here. *What* are you doing? We thought you'd gone on a cruise.'

Dulcie shivered and tore up another letter but kept it tight in her fist, staring ahead.

'You are – Dulcie, you are not *still* writing to Fiscal-Smith!'

'Trying to. He hasn't answered *any* of them. It's weeks and weeks. He doesn't seem to be on the phone or have this email thing. Neither do I. Nearly a month and no thank-you letter. It's unheard of. It's not that I want to see him, it's just so out of character. And this great pink and gold chair is waiting for him. Wrapped in tarpaulin. When a friend of sixty years begins to act out of character you begin to wonder if you might never ... There's nobody up there – it's called Lone Hall – nobody to contact. I don't think it's anywhere near a police station ...'

'Oh, I'm sure the postman can find it.'

'Anna, I was very cruel to him. I let him know that we had always thought him mean and grasping. All his life he's been longing for company and nobody has wanted him because he's, well, so awful, really. So disgracefully conceited. Clever, of course. Efficient. But withdrawn and obscure. But – oh Anna! – he's always been *there*. He has no charm and he knows it. Can't connect. Can't hear people thinking. Can't *help* being what he is. He knows that nobody ever liked him. Haven't I a *duty* to him, Anna?'

'Certainly not!'

'But I *do*. He's broken the pattern. The cracks will spread. They'll spread across all our crumbling lives, the few of us who are left.'

'Oh, come on, Dulcie.'

'He's disappeared, Anna. It isn't senility, and it isn't spite or resentment because we've laughed at him all these years. It's simple, determined rejection of us, of the very, very few last friends. Where *is* he, Anna?'

'Come home with me. We'll find out. Get your things – not the ones on the floor – and stay the night. I'm not leaving you here alone. You've got no tights on. No shoes. Your feet are navy blue.'

'Oh, but I don't do that sort of thing. Stay with people, if it's not in the diary.'

'You're coming.'

*

'Hi, Dulcie,' said Henry, holding Sellotape and a shoe. 'All well?'

'It's not,' said Anna, and gave a résumé.

'Well, OK then,' he said. 'I'm off up North tomorrow, Dulcie. I'm lecturing on the Cavalier Poets at Teesside University. It's about ten miles from Yarm. I'll fix up the famous Judges Hotel, Execution Court or whatever, for you to stay the night. I'm staying with the Dean at Acklam and a few Cavaliers, but you'll be well looked after at the Judges, by all accounts. Then next morning we'll visit the mandarin's marble hall on the blasted heath and thunder on his door. Then we'll come home. That very evening. I'll – Anna will – ring the hotel now.'

'Oh, but I couldn't possibly! I don't travel any more, you know. I haven't had my hair done. And – Anna – I'm afraid I have to get up in the night now, you know. I'd never find my way back to my room in an hotel.'

'They have things called "en suite" now, Dulcie.'

'Oh, but I try not to eat them.'

'RIGHT,' shouted Henry returning to his pizza and pesto at the supper table, children munching and doing homework. 'All fixed. Hotel's got a room. Sounds rather an odd one but apparently the great Old Filth once slept there. Probably Judge Jeffries, too. It's en suite and much in demand. I said I'd take you up to the Fiscalry first and then see you in and make sure you'll get a good dinner, and then I'll pick you up the following morning and bring you home. All right?'

Anna said, 'I'll go up to Privilege House now and get anything you're going to need. Pills? Shoes? No. Be quiet. You're going.'

'But, it's hundreds of miles and—'

'Hong Kong is thousands.'

'Oh, but I *know* Hong Kong. And actually, Anna, I'm afraid I'm not very reliable on the motorway.'

'You won't be driving.'

'No, my dear, I mean the facilities. I would have to stop at least twice.'

'Me too,' said Henry. 'Always did. Don't boast. We'll be on the road by eight o'clock. Could you manage that?'

'I wake at four,' said Dulcie proudly.

'And *you* go upstairs and finish that lecture *now*,' said Anna.

'But there are other things,' said Dulcie. 'I have to check on Filth's house.'

'There've been lights on,' said Anna. 'Someone's taking care of it.'

It was very early when Isobel heard the hired car arrive at Filth's garden gate.

She put on her long silk coat, noticed that it was raining, noticed Filth's old mac hanging on the back of the kitchen door. But no, she'd take nothing. She had everything she wanted (the house she would leave to the boy – old Dulcie's grandson), for Filth had given her everything, not only his worldly possessions but his living spirit.

She pressed her face briefly against the cold waterproof on the door and left the house. On quick feet, without a stick, she climbed up the slope of the garden to the waiting taxi.

By 8.15 the poet's car was heading North, Dulcie crouched like a marmoset in the back, defying whiplash, her eyes pools of fear. By the motorway, however, she had settled and started the *Telegraph* crossword. After a stop at a service station, cross-country towards Nottingham she began to take notice. By lunchtime, when they stopped at a country-house hotel

Henry had known from literary festivals before, she had a light in her eyes and was talking about the landscape of D. H. Lawrence and the Mitford sisters and Chatsworth. Soon she appeared to have blood in her veins again and was chatting up the austere black waiter over the cheese, telling him of Arbitrations in Africa, where he had never been.

'Now – *I* am paying for this,' Dulcie said and blinked when she saw the bill, holding it up first one way and then the other. A deep breath – then, '*Oh* yes. I am paying, and I am leaving the tip.' She put down a pound coin. 'Henry, this is wonderful. We must do this again and I will pay the petrol. Are you doing the Edinburgh Festival in August?'

It was already dark by the time they reached Yarm. Henry's lecture was at eight o' clock. 'I'll ring the hotel and say to keep dinner for you. We'll go up to Fiscal-Smith's for a quick look now. I'll make sure your room will be ready when I drop you back. Here we are, here's the Fiscal turning. *Hup* we go to Wuthering Heights. God! There's nothing!'

The steep lane ran on and up, up and on, white with moonlight, black with wintry heather. Lying to either side of it, and occasionally on it, the green lamp-eyes of sheep. A few ('Oh, *look*,' she cried) new lambs with bewildered faces. Henry honked and tooted and the sheep ambled aside.

Down they went again, into a village with a noisy stream, a small stone bridge, arched high. Up they went again, twist and twirl, and the stars were coming out.

'Such stars!' she said. 'And I thought the Donheads were the country!'

'You can see the Milky Way,' he said. 'They say it's disappeared now over London. We've blotted it out.'

'I don't remember stars in Hong Kong,' she said. 'It's such a competitive place.'

'Aha!' he said.

A gate across a track.

'Henry – turn! You're going to be late. It's seven o' clock. We can come back tomorrow on the way home.'

'Won't be beaten,' he shouted, getting out, opening the gate, dragging it wide for the return journey, jumping back in, splashing the car through another rattling torrent. Over a narrow bridge came a sharp bend upwards, a one-in-three corkscrew, and a shriek from Dulcie. The car made it with only a foot to spare along the edge of a dark brackeny precipice.

'The man's a madman,' said Henry, 'living here. Oh – hello?'

Mist had been gathering but now, up here, moonlight broke through and in front of them was another barred gate. Behind it stood a man in silhouette, carrying what looked like a pitchfork or perhaps a rifle. To either side of his head swayed the great horns of two wild beasts. Henry stopped the car once more and waited to see if the gate would roll back.

'So what's this then?' shouted the man.

'Visitors.'

'Visitors! This time of night? It's past six o'clock. Are you daft? Mek an appointment.'

'*Visitors*. To Sir Frederick Fiscal-Smith.'

'Fred's out. I'm his ghillie. And these are two of his Highlanders.'

'*Out?*'

'Aye. An' 'e's not comin' back. Hall's for sale. He's gone to Hong Kong.'

Dulcie stepped carefully out of the car and went over to the gate. She held out her hand to the ghillie. The wild beasts disappeared into the mist. 'I am so sorry,' she said, 'to descend upon you in the dark, and we must go at once – there is a very important engagement. A poetry lecture in Middles-brough. On *the Cavalier Poets*. But I just wanted to look in on my very old friend. I *quite* understand. We hadn't realised that Sir – Sir Fred's house was so remote. Might I just come and take another look tomorrow? Could I just have a look in the letterbox?'

'*Letterbox?* Nothing of that sort up here. The letters get dropped down the bottom. Under a stone. I've been posting on yeller envelopes, but I send them by the batch. Not straight off. You can't catch the postman. You know, our Fred were always a mystery.'

'I'll have to abandon you,' said Henry at the Judges Hotel. 'I'll be back to take you home after breakfast. I'll have to step on it now. Here's someone.'

An amiable man in porter's uniform was hanging about. He disappeared with Dulcie's case and in a moment came a strong-looking woman down the steps. She had the air of someone who had seen too many hotel guests from the South.

When she spoke, however, all was well. 'Hot water, hot-water bottles and your dinner's ready in half an hour and you can tek the same room as the others had. We seem to get more judges than we ever did when they was on circuit. Poor old Feathers crying into his coffee after his wife died. Fiscal-Smith up the hill, he nearly died, in the room you're having, not six weeks ago. Pneumonia. Well, two memorial services in a few months. He can't resist a train ride to London ...'

Henry said, 'He's in Hong Kong now.'

'Doesn't surprise me. Now, you get off to your poetry and we'll get this one installed.'

Lying in the lights from the bedside lamp, Dulcie was early in bed. She watched the goldfish as they flicked and turned.

*

And seated at breakfast in the dining room, looking up into the frowning hills, Dulcie was smiling. Susan – not any one of them – knew where she was. There was no one who would be screeching at her on a telephone to say that this journey had been foolish. 'Sheer bravado!' 'Showing off.' 'At your age,' and so on. Such an interesting visit up to the moors last night. *Such* a good hotel! Black pudding for breakfast. Delicious.

Here came the manageress.

'Oh, yes, *perfectly* thank you. I slept perfectly. I wish I could stay here for a proper holiday.'

'Well, it's possible,' said the lady – more coffee was being hustled to the table, unasked. 'In fact it's inevitable. There's bin a message . . . '

'Yes?' (Oh God! Oh God, it's Susan!)

'From the University. Your friend – that poet – he's in Great North Eastern Hospital with a broken ankle.'

'He's *what*?'

'Slipped as he came off stage last night after his lecture. Shoe fell to pieces, got caught up in the audio wires. Foot left hanging like a leaf. They'se hoping to operate this morning.'

'I must go there at once. *At once!*'

'Have some more coffee. They've informed the wife and she's on't train. We'll go to Darlington to meet her. She'll drive you back home tomorrow but – something about arrangements for the school run. I said that we'd see to you.'

'Oh, but I must go to poor Henry!'

'He won't be round from his anaesthetic yet. They may not even operate today. He's high blood-pressure.'

'That doesn't surprise me. Could you get me a car? I haven't got my actual driver's licence with me. I haven't driven for quite some time, except around the village. But someone might lend me a map. I do thoroughly enjoy driving. I could drive Anna home – or just go by myself.'

'Michael will drive you to the hospital whenever you need to go.'

'Is he the ghillie?' I'm not sure . . .'

'No. He's over there. The front-of-house receptionist standing by the portrait of Lord Justice Grampian. Drinking milk.'

Michael gave a little wave.

'The milk,' the manageress said, 'is a bit eccentric, but it's a good fault in a driver. Yes, it's hard to get insurance when you're over eighty. I hope I don't speak out of turn?'

'Oh, I can easily take a taxi just to the hospital.'

'They're not going to want you at the hospital, my lady. You're not next of kin. But where would you like Michael to tek you? Is there someone you can visit?'

'Oh no. I don't know a living soul. Oh – oh yes, I must ring my daughter Susan. In America. But perhaps, well – no. She is rather easily annoyed. Though a *wonderful* person. Quite wonderful. Do you think – would it be possible to visit Lone Hall again?'

'There's a call for you.'

'Yes? Oh, Anna! Anna, *yes*, I'm very well.'

'Dulcie. I'm on the train. The silly great fool.'

'Who?'

'Henry.'

'Now don't worry about me, Anna. I'm perfectly all right. I was often stuck in Ethiopia, you know (that road across the Blue Mountains). I do just wonder if I left the iron on. But we must think of Henry first.'

'I'll have to get Henry home. I'll bring you back with him. I'm afraid he may be in rather a dreadful mood.'

'All will be perfectly well, Anna, and could you possibly ring Susan in Massachusetts in case she worries? You have the number. I'm going to drive about today with a splendid young man and we'll leave some flowers for Henry though it's still very wintry up here – bring a big coat – and there's nothing but black heather. Oh, yes. Fiscal-Smith? I'd forgotten him. He's not here. He's gone to Hong Kong. I was mistaken ever to have worried about him.'

'And now,' she said, 'young man, come along. They say you'll get me to the hospital.'

'I'll get you there,' he said, 'but I can't say what we'll do next. It's like a city. They made it out of the old chemical works. They were the steelworks before that and the ironworks before that and before that they were the Big Wilderness. Kept thousands working for a hundred years. Always work. Dirt and clatter. All gone now. Most folks have no jobs. They just lay in bed most days, unless they have a profession, like me.'

'But this hospital's enormous! There must be plenty of jobs here?'

'Oh, aye. Mind, how many *does* any work in it? D'you want a bit of Cadbury's Fruit and Nut?'

'So very different from Dorset. And from Hong Kong. We'll never find poor Henry here,' she said.

But a car park appeared and someone to take her to the ward where the family man and poet lay with eyes closed and mind elsewhere. She felt affection for him and stroked his face.

'He didn't speak,' she said when she came back. 'I left him a packet of Smarties.'

'Hey ho,' said Michael. 'So where now?'

'Well. I suppose back to the hotel.'

'No – come on. I'll show you Herringfleet. First we'll go to Whitby for its fish and chips and I can get blue-top. Then there's the museum with the preserved mermaid – mind, she's not that well preserved, being dead. We'll take the trunk road through the skeletal chimneys. They're not that old,' he said.

'Younger than me! Mind, not much. Can't think of the place without them now.'

'You were born here then, Michael?'

'Oh, aye. Michael Watkins. Me great-auntie was Nurse Watkins. Gypsy stock. Black eyes. Delivered us all and laid us all out. She delivered your great man, Judge Varenski or whatever . . .'

'I'm afraid I don't know . . . ?'

'Changed his name and went South. Something you could spell more easier. Me Great-Auntie Watkins knew 'em all. His mother worked the coal cart round the streets. His dad were a Russian spy. Common knowledge.'

'You *can't*,' she said, 'mean Judge Veneering?'

'It could be,' said Michael. 'They're all dead now. Here then – Whitby. Home of Dracula and a load a' saints. And, see them choppers on't clifftop? Visiting whale. Made *Jaws* look like a minner. And here's a human hand of some lass hanged somewhere. Stick a candle in it and you'll never be frightened of ghosts.'

'There's nothing like this in Hong Kong,' she said. 'Though I wouldn't answer for Java. In Java they keep the bodies of the dead for years. They take them food.'

'Well there you are then,' said Michael. 'It's a funny old world. What you think of this? Look up, now.'

Hanging on wires from the museum's roof glimmered a painted wooden banner, pale green and gold. Trailing squirls and tendrils of delicate foreign flowers surrounded lettering she couldn't decipher.

'It's wonderful. What is it? What does it say?'

'Nobody can make out. But it's not that old.'

'It looks almost Classical.'

'No. It was something from Muriel Street. The street was flattened with a bomb and this thing somehow survived.'

'It looks as old as *The Odyssey*.'

'Aye, it's odd all right. Kind of sadness in it too. Horrible back alley it hung in. They used to slaughter cattle there on a Thursday.'

She looked at him. 'I'm not a complete *ingénue*, Michael.'

'The guy painted that,' said Michael, 'wasn't no jane-you neither. He was like a god. But he was broken up. He was that Varenski's dad. The Russian spy.'

'I'm out of my depth, Michael.' She took his arm.

'Who isn't?' said Michael.

'And,' she said back in the car, 'you've lived here all your life? How very interesting.'

'I've had some foreign holidays. Now, before we set off back, tek a look down there. Look around.'

'Sea?' she said. 'It's rather pale – if you saw the Caribbean, Michael . . . '

'Look along the coastline. Right? All ripped off in the war. The big raid took the heart out of it. See that yellow house with the black holes for windows? Never rebuilt. Streets of little dwellings down the old High Street. All gone. I never seed 'em. Ripped away like the flounce on a skirt, me auntie says. Bessie Bell. She's still alive. D'you want to meet her?'

'Well, I think we should get back.'

'You've to see Grangetown. Ugliest place, it's said, in Europe. Covered in red dust off the old ironstone works. It crosses the sea on the wind. They say Denmark's covered in it. It's on a level with Ayers Rock, Australia. D'you know, they used these beaches for filming D-Day? In that film. Nowhere in France poor enough. Number three hundred and twenty-six Palm Tree Road, here's Auntie's. She's near a hundred, too. I'll get her.'

Dulcie sat alone in the car. The long, long street of tiny

houses was by no means derelict or poor but it was lifeless. Rebuilt since the war, dozen after dozen, all alike. Well kept, anonymous, identical. Curtains were pasted against the windows. No one to be seen. Concrete and weeds in the long, long vista of tiny front gardens. Silence. No people. On every house a satellite dish. Then a boy with small eyes came up beside the car and spat at it.

After a while a shuffling old man with a dog appeared, stopping and looking, looking and stopping. He put his face near hers at the passenger window and said through the glass, 'Is it Lilian?'

'No, I'm Dulcie.'

'I'm looking out for our Lilian. She's seldom coming by.'

'I'm sorry.'

'I'd say the Germans have her.'

'That was a *very* long time ago.'

'Behind that Iron Curtain.'

'That was a long time ago, too.'

'No, it were yesterday. Not even the blacks come here, you know. Too dismal for 'em. Our Lilian was a grand girl.'

Michael came down his aunt's concrete path and said Dulcie was to come in. 'And you get on with your walk,' he said to the man.

'Michael, this old man is crying. For his sister.'

'Oh aye. Lilian. Half a century on. Killed in Middlesbrough bombing. Shut up now, George. There was worse going on than Lilian. What about the concentration camps?'

'It's all stood still,' said the old man.

'Aye, and that's the trouble,' said Michael.

As Dulcie pulled on her little mohair gloves, as she walked up the path, the old man shouted, 'It was wireless won us t'war. If it had been only bloody television we'd have lost it and mebbe got some soul back in us. It went out, did soul, with Churchill. We was all listening to him when the Dorniers come that night.'

A woman was watching them from the doorstep.

'Are you comin' in then?'

She didn't look a hundred, she looked fifty and very alert.

'Friends o' Terry's? Terry Venetski? Cup o' tea?'

'I'm afraid Terry is gone,' said Dulcie, drawing off her gloves, Bessie watching, stretching over and taking one and stroking it. 'I went to his memorial service. He died in Malta.'

'What in heck was he doing there? He was that restless. Is't true he married a Chinese?'

'Yes. Elsie. I hardly knew her ... '

'Now then, tell us. One thing we can still do here is talk. I wonder if she was like his mother, Florrie. Now she was a fine woman, like a man. With a back-to-front man's cap. Here's your tea and a fancy. It's only shop.'

'They – didn't exactly get on. Terry and Elsie.'

'Then there'd be someone else. Terry was born to love women. Serviette? You can't see where he lived. Nowt left. Nowt much left of Florrie neither, nor the Russian. Eighty-seven killed that night. Terry was out of it, you know, because they'd put him on some getaway train that afternoon. He left without a tear. I helped get his mother home where she'd been waving at the train from the fence. Oh, she was a fine woman. She never knew if he'd seen her waving.'

'And you've never moved away?'

'Well, bus trips with Michael, in a club, to foreign parts but I can't recommend them. Up here's better, even with the drugs and the knives – even in *Turner* Street! Turner Street where the doctors used to live and the manager of the Co-op. Even now it's better than the Costa del Sol where you can't under-stand a word they say. All those fat English women, they're a disgrace. I was maid at a posh school here once, you know. That was a nasty place, but interesting and you never saw anything like that Mrs Fondle in her purples and satins. She fancied young Terry. Yes she did. Just as well she got drowned. There was tensions all right, what with Mrs Fondle and circus performers and spies and coal carts – bit of Dundee? I mek me own Dundee.'

'It must have been a very – very vivid time,' said Dulcie. 'I was in Shanghai about then. It was really my country. I don't know why we were all so mad on this one we'd never seen.'

'I'd not think Shanghai would have been all water-lilies and flowers-behind-the-ear neither. But, like wherever you go, there's great compensations. Great people.'

'Oh – yes.'

'Like Mr Parable in Herringfleet. Now *he* was mad. He was what's called a religious maniac but he was one of the nicest men you could hope to meet. I wonder where his money went?'

'And then,' she said, 'there was that Mr Smith. He had a son, too. Tight-up little chap. Never very taking. Father took no note of him but they say he did well, mebbe better than Terry. But yet, with little Fred, nobody ever seemed to take to him.'

'Yes. I see. It's another world to me, you know. You make me feel very *narrow*, Mrs . . .'

'Miss,' she said. 'Thank God.'

There was a silence, Dulcie thinking of all the countries she had lived in where nobody now cared for her one jot, Bessie thinking of the children of this grey place who had shone here once. 'Did you say our Terry's *gone*?' she asked, and Dulcie said again she had been to his memorial service. 'We don't go in for that round here,' said Bessie, 'whoever you are. It's York Minster if you're someone, but otherwise it's Mr Davison at

Herringfleet Church digging a hole. And we don't go for these basketwork caskets neither. Remind you of the old laundry down Cargo Fleet. I suppose little Fred's gone too.'

'Thank you,' Dulcie said to the milk-drinking Michael on the way back from the sea to the Cleveland Hills.

'Pretty great, in't she?'

'What a memory.'

'Aye, but Dulcie – what a terrible life.'

'Michael, I don't think so. Oh good! Look.' For here was the Donhead car in the forecourt of the hotel. 'Oh thank God! She's back from the hospital. Now we can go home.'

Chapter Twenty-two

But the next morning they were both still at the hotel. Henry was being kept in hospital for another day and arrangements had to be made for an ambulance.

'We'll drive in convoy,' said Anna, 'you and I in the car. It'll be rather slow. But more restful than the journey up. Today I'll go to the hospital and see the surgeon and arrange about physio. But what will *you* do?'

'I'll go to Lone Hall again.'

'But you said it was grim.'

'Yes. But I can't stop thinking about him all alone in it.'

'I hope you're not thinking of joining him in it?'

'Don't be ridiculous, Anna. I shouldn't tell you this, but I can't really afford Privilege House any more, and it's in very good condition. This one needs a million pounds spending on it. Dear Anna – it's idle curiosity, that's all. Could they get me a lift up there and back, d'you think? The hotel?'

They could. She did. The ghillie was on his way up there now. He was meeting a possible buyer.

'But would he let me in?' she said. 'I want to go round it alone.'

'Dulcie?'

'I tell you, Fiscal-Smith's not there. He's gone to Hong Kong.'

'Look – it has nothing to do with you where Fiscal-Smith lives. He's only there because he can't shake off his childhood. That's why he's such a *bore*, Dulcie. You deserve better. Fiscal-Smith clings to his miserable past like a limpet to a rock.'

'I don't think anyone has ever loved him,' she said.

'I'm not surprised.'

'Anna, you are being unpleasant. Fiscal-Smith is pathetic because he doesn't know how to love. But there's a For Sale notice up and this time – he never tells you anything – something must have happened. I believe, Anna, that he's a virgin.'

'I hope you're not thinking of doing something about that.'

'That will do, Anna. We don't talk like that. And I'd be glad if you'd tell *nobody* that I'm short of money.'

'Oh – ah! Well, well – Fiscal-Smith's worth millions, just like the other two. *Now* I understand!'

'I hope we are not about to quarrel, Anna.'

The ghillie dropped her off and she was allowed to go alone into the gaunt, wind-blown house on the moor.

'I'm glad you trust me,' she said as he handed her a key the size of a rolling-pin.

'I can tell a good woman,' he said. 'Ye'll not pilfer. And it suits me because I have to wait outside for the estate agents. They're bringing in a possible buyer. Some lunatic. I'll look him over. Off ye go now and mind ye take care on the boards.'

'Is it clean?' she said.

'Och, aye, it's clean.'

Inside Fiscal-Smith's Lone Hall, the smell of wood fires and heather. No carpets, no curtains and very little furniture. A kitchen range like a James Watt steam engine, rusted and ice-cold, a midget microwave beside it, an electric toaster, almost antique. Taps high above a yellow stone sink, and an empty larder. An empty bread-crock, a calendar of years ago marked with crosses indicating absences abroad. All colourless, clean, scrubbed. Eighteenth-centry windows, light flowing in from moor and sky.

Where did he sleep? Where did he eat? Where did he read – whatever did he *do* here? Room after room: empty. Not a painting, not a clock, not a photograph.

On her way out she opened a door on the ground floor behind a shabby baize curtain. The room within was cold – another tall window, unshuttered, the walls covered with shelves and upon them row upon row of boxes, all neatly labelled. There was a man's bike with a flowing leather saddle and a round silver bell. It stood upside-down. A very old basket was strapped to the handlebars. On a hook nearby was a dingy white riding-mackintosh with brass eyelet holes under the arms. It hung stiff as wood. There was a black, tinny filing cabinet labelled EXAMINATION PAPERS. No sign anywhere of a woman's presence, or touch.

There was a complete set of English Law Reports in leather, worth several thousands of pounds – Dulcie knew this because she had recently decided to sell Willy's. There was an iron bed, like the campaign bed of the Duke of Wellington. Beside the bed a missal, its pages loose with wear. Then she saw, on the wall behind her, a photograph of familiar faces. Willy waving. Herself in a rose-scattered hat – my, wasn't I gorgeous! Those tiresome missionaries in Iran. Eddie Feathers, magnificent in full-bottomed wig. Veneering cracking up with laughter, hold-ing golf clubs, hair flying. Drunk.

Row after row of them and no girlfriends, no children, no one who could have been Fred's invisible, ailing mother.

In the dead centre of the collage was a wedding group outside St James's Church, Hong Kong. Eddie Feathers, so young and almost ridiculously good-looking in his old-fashioned morning suit and bridegroom's camellia; the bride Elisabeth – darling Betty – in frothy lace, with a face looking out like a baby at its christening.

And there, beside Betty, astonishingly in a T-shirt and what must have been the first pair of jeans in the Colony, was Fiscal-Smith, the super-careful conformist, never wrongly dressed. Asked to be best man at the last minute. His face was shining like the Holy Ghost. The best day of his life.

No sign of Veneering in this photograph. No sign at all. Nor of Isobel Ingoldby, the femme fatale.

Willy was there. Oh, look at us, look at us! Still damp from our cocoons!

But it was the huge floor of the same room in Lone Hall that held Dulcie now. It was slung from end to end with swathes of tiny metal Hornby rolling-stock: points, buffers, level crossings, signals, water pumps, platforms, sheds, long seats, lacy wooden canopies, slot machines; luggage trolleys like floats with unbending metal handles long as cart-shafts. Portmanteaux, trunks, Gladstone bags, sacks red and grey, and all set up for midgets. And calm, good midgets stood in dark blue uniforms blowing pinhead whistles, punching pinholes in tiny tickets. Branch lines were slung far and wide, under the Duke of Wellington's bed, and were criss-crossed by bridges, paralleled by streams where tiny men in floppy hats sat fishing. And the station platforms, up and down the room, were decorated with tiny tubs of geraniums. Time had stopped.

In the green-painted fields around lived happy sheep and lambs and cardboard figures carrying ladders over their shoulders, and pots of paint. They went smiling to their daily bread. And the engines! And the goods wagons! And the carriages upholstered in blue and red and green velvets. And the happy pin-sized families untouched by care, all loving each other.

There was someone else in the house. The ghillie was at the door. He was furious. 'This room is not on view. You are here without permission,' and he locked the door behind her as she fled.

Another car, a Mercedes, was on the drive now, with the estate agent kowtowing, and she heard someone say, 'Very sad. Hong Kong businessman. Made his pile. No, no – a local. Not in residence at present but lived here for years. Matter of fact, we've just heard he has recently died – back in Hong Kong.'

'Good afternoon,' said Dulcie as she passed.

'So sorry about your wasted journey,' called the man with the shooting-stick. 'I've bought it already. Fixtures and fittings. Splendid shooting-lodge. I'd better not tell you how cheap it was.'

And he stood aside, laughing, and watched her climb sadly into the ghillie's car.

The next day she was driving South with Anna to the Donheads, the ambulance somewhere behind them, cautiously bouncing and now and then sounding its siren.

'They wanted to keep him in longer, Dulcie; oh, I wish they had! He's going to be hell downstairs at home. Physios coming in three times a day – on the good old NHS of course – and pray God they're pretty. Oh – and he'll be surrounded by the yellow staircase! Oh help me, Dulcie.'

'I suppose – did you hear anything about the lecture?'

'Brilliant, of course. The wilder the preliminaries the better he always seems to be.'

'It's not like that in lawsuits.'

In time: 'Dulcie? You're very quiet. You did want to come back home, I hope?'

'Yes. I did. I do. All is settled now.'

'I'm so sorry. We messed it all up for you. It was meant to be a treat. We're so disorganised.'

'Anna, stop it. You have taken the leathery old scales from my eyes and I love you both.'

'Why?'

'Well, I've rather gone in for romantic secrets in other people's lives. "Romantic" is not quite right. It's a dirty word now, meaning sexy and silly. But, for me, it has always meant imaginative and beautiful and private. By the way, did I tell you that poor Fiscal-Smith is dead?'

The car swerved and swung in an arc from the fast lane to the central to the slow and stopped with a screech of brakes on the hard shoulder. Traffic swore at them.

'Dulcie! *What*—?'

'Yes. Fiscal-Smith is dead. I overheard up at the Hall. A rather awful man has bought it. He shouted at me.'

'Oh, Dulcie! It *can't* be true. He was perfectly all right at Old Filth's party – I mean memorial service. Who the *hell* are these morbid Northern lunatics? I'll email Hong Kong. Where was he staying? The Peninsular, of course.'

'Not if he was paying the bill himself. No, Anna. It would have been the YMCA. He liked it there. Maybe I should go out. At once.'

'You do not *stir*, Dulcie. Not till we have the facts.'

'I think I may. I think you've given me the urge to travel again, Anna. Oh, I do hope that at least some of my letters got there in time. I'm afraid I was very outspoken though. I apologised rather pathetically – I don't really know why. I said too much. But actually – I don't think one *can* say too much at my time of life, do you? Or ever. About love.'

'I'm sorry, Dulcie. I just don't believe he's dead.' And they drove on for many miles.

'Life,' said Dulcie, south of Birmingham, 'is really ridiculous. Why were we thought worth creating if we are such bloody fools? What's happiness? I wish I could talk to Susan like this.'

'Well, you can't. The idea that mothers and daughters can say everything to each other is a myth. But I know she loves you. In her way.'

'That makes me feel better. But, Anna – why does it *have* to be "in her way"?'

They turned off at last into the unlikely lane off the A30 towards the Donheads and Dulcie found herself pointing out to dear, dead Betty Feathers the tree in the hedge that looked like a huge hen on a nest. And the funny man – look, he *is* still there! – who wanders about with a scythe. (He won't go into care, you know. I can't say I blame him. I'm going to stick on as long as I can at Privilege House, even if I have to sell the spoons.)

'Here we are, Dulcie. I'm going to stop here and wait for the ambulance. It's not far behind. Here it comes. Marvellous!'

'And I'm getting out here,' said Dulcie, 'if you'll get my pull-along out of the back. Yes – yes, I mean it. You must go with Henry. I'll walk to my front gate – you can see it from here, look.'

'I'll ring up in half an hour,' said Anna. 'And I'll watch you in. We'll bring you some supper. Soon. *Now don't forget*, turn and wave at the gate.'

Dulcie trailed her case on wheels to the wrought-iron gate, which she was surprised to see open, and turned and waved.

Then she turned back towards the courtyard, where Fiscal-Smith was standing surrounded by an enormous amount of luggage.

Chapter Twenty-three

It was Easter Day. St Ague's bells were clanking out and the steep church path was at its most slippery and dangerous. Filth's magnificent legacy was still being discussed. And discussed. What first? Heating, roof, floor, walls, glass, pews, *path*? In the mean time, in spring, the clumps of primroses would go on growing like bridesmaids' bouquets in the nooks and crannies of the old railway-sleeper steps. Dulcie and Fred were proceeding cautiously towards the Easter Eucharist and, on every side, tulips and daffodils and pansies graced the graves for Easter, in pots and jars and florists' confections.

'It's like a fruit salad,' said Fiscal-Smith. 'I don't care for it. Never did. Pagan.'

'Oh, "live and let . . . "' said Dulcie. 'But no. That's not very apt.'

'I want these railway sleepers out,' said Fiscal-Smith. 'They're black and full of slugs. We can get good money for them. Install proper steps! There's a church I've heard of in south Dorset where they've put in a lift and an escalator. I'll have to get on to it.'

'You're a Roman Catholic, Fiscal-Smith. St Ague's is nothing to do with you.'

'Wait till I'm on the Parish Council,' he said. 'Dulcie! Stand clear. Here's that Chloe.'

Chloe rushed by them, carrying chocolate rabbits for after the service.

'On, on,' he said. 'End in sight. Doors wide open. Or we could construct a sort of polytunnel.'

A gold haze hung inside the church door. Lilies. Tall candles, a glinting cope. 'Don't fuss – they can't start without us,' he said. And Dulcie said, 'What rubbish.'

They had to pause again. In the porch could be seen the gleam of one of the twins' walking-frames and the carer skulking round the back of a tombstone, having a quick drag on a Gauloise.

'The gravestones are a disgrace too,' said Fiscal-Smith. 'Tipping about. I can see to that. The most useful thing I've learned in my long career at the construction-industry Bar is the importance of a reliable builder.'

'I like them tipping about,' she said.

'I knew a man *killed* by a gravestone tipping about,' said Fiscal-Smith.

'I expect it was trying to tell him something. Just listen to Old Filth's rooks! They're back again.'

'Were they ever away?' he said.

'Fred – the organ! It's *roaring*. The procession's gathering up for "The Fight is O'er, the Battle Done". Come *on*. Wonderful! Hurry!'

'Reminds me of old Eddie's wedding day in Hong Kong,' he said. 'I don't know if you remember, Dulcie, but he chose me to be his best man.'

'Were there no *girls* in your life, Fred?'

Arm in arm, they tottered.

'Just you, Dulcie. Otherwise I'm afraid it was only trains.'

Singing mingled with the flooding thunder of the organ. 'Calm, my dear,' said Fiscal-Smith. 'Calm.'

And so they made their way towards the Resurrection.

Acknowledgements

Thanks, as ever, to my friends and publishers Richard Beswick of Little, Brown and Abacus, and Kent Carroll of Europeditions, New York.

And, yet again, to my editor Penelope Hoare who tells me firmly when I am incomprehensible and when my modern history is awry, and how 'just a tweak' (often a wrench) will put things right. Any mistakes remaining are my own. Thanks too to Heather Hall who typed the manuscript with calm and fortitude, and has been general midwife to this gang of ghosts. And particularly to Ania Corless, who put me straight about Poland, Russia and Odessa after the war.

And thanks to Tom Nagorski who wrote the story of the torpedoing by U-boats of the SS *City of Benares* in September 1940. It is an unflinching account of the two hundred passengers, ninety of them child evacuees, who drowned on their way to safety in Canada to escape the London Blitz. *Miracles on the Water* is one of the 'great lost stories of WWII' (Robinson Publishing, 2006).

Thanks again to Richard Ingrams who asked me for a

Christmas story for *The Oldie* in 2004. Old Filth (Sir Edward Feathers) has become my alter ego, and this year has made it to clue 25 across in the *Times Literary Supplement* crossword!

Jane Gardam is the only writer to have been twice awarded the Whitbread/Costa Prize for Best Novel of the Year, for *The Queen of the Tambourine* and *The Hollow Land*. She also holds a Heywood Hill Literary Prize for a lifetime's contribution to the enjoyment of literature. She is the author of four volumes of acclaimed stories: *Black Faces, White Faces* (David Higham Prize and the Royal Society for Literature's Winifred Holtby Prize); *The Pangs of Love* (Katherine Mansfield Prize); *Going into a Dark House* (Silver Pen Award from PEN); and *Missing the Midnight*.

Her novels include *God on the Rocks*, which was shortlisted for the Booker Prize; *Faith Fox*; *The Flight of the Maidens*; the bestselling *Old Filth*, which was shortlisted for the Orange Prize in 2005; *The People on Privilege Hill*; and, most recently, *The Man in the Wooden Hat*.

Jane Gardam was born in Yorkshire, travelled often in the Far East and now lives in east Kent.